Love, Lies and Butterflies

Christine Skippins

Published by The Book Dragon, 2025.

This is a work of fiction. Similarities to real people, places, or events are entirely coincidental.

LOVE, LIES AND BUTTERFLIES

First edition. September 1, 2025.

Copyright © 2025 Christine Skippins.

ISBN: 978-1917608206

Written by Christine Skippins.

Table of Contents

Chapter One – Divorce 1
Chapter Two – Getting Back Out There............................... 4
Chapter Three – Finding Love 9
Chapter Four – What's Mine is Yours, and What's Yours is Mine..20
Chapter Five - Cyprus or Bust 33
Chapter Six – All That Glistens is Not Gold......................43
Chapter Seven – A Twisted Web 56
Chapter Eight – Barry Brown..62
Chapter Nine – Embracing the Chaos 71
Chapter Ten – The Investigation...79
Chapter Eleven – The Sting..87
Chapter Twelve – And Suddenly 95
Chapter Thirteen – Hidden in Plain Sight 105
Chapter Fourteen – And So the Cards Tumble...............112
Chapter Fifteen – Reflections and Ripples 119
Chapter Sixteen – Too Much Too Soon............................129
Chapter Seventeen – Back to Square One. 136
Chapter Eighteen – 'Jolie Retraite' 142
Chapter Nineteen – Château Anaïs Day One 149
Chapter Twenty – Château Anaïs Day Two.....................159
Chapter Twenty-One – Living the Dream 166
Chapter Twenty-Two - The Court of the Pen 172
Chapter Twenty-Three – This Writing Life 181
Chapter Twenty-Four – The Next Turning on the Road to Rediscovery 190
Chapter Twenty-Five – Learning From the Past 205
Chapter Twenty-Six – Family Time...................................209

Chapter Twenty-Seven – The Adventure is the Journey, Not the Destination 215
Chapter Twenty-Eight - Pieces of a Puzzle 222

Dedication

To everyone who feels that they have a story in them, and to all those who have stood by me as I ventured to share mine.

To my incredible family: your belief in me and your encouragement to chase my creative dreams have been the wind beneath my wings. Thank you for being my steadfast supporters.

To my amazing friends, especially Karen—your unwavering support in both writing and promoting my work has been a beacon of light on this journey. Your faith in me is a constant reminder that dreams are meant to be pursued.

Inspiration surrounds us, woven into the fabric of our lives, and each of you has contributed to the depth and richness of my characters.

Lastly, my heartfelt gratitude goes to my professional inspirations, Kirsty and Michelle, and the incredible team at The Book Dragon. Your guidance and expertise have propelled me forward.

A special thank you also to JR Caines from JR Caines Design for your creative vision, which supported me in embarking on my writing journey.

Thank you all for being part of my story.

Friends and lovers come into our lives for a reason, a season, or for life.

PROLOGUE – CYPRUS, JANUARY 2018

THE HOTEL ROOM FEELS hollow, and my suitcase is still unpacked in the corner. Outside, the Mediterranean sunset turns the sky amber, and the cicadas sing, but I can't appreciate its beauty. I check my phone for what feels like the thousandth time. There is still no message from James.

I've been here four days, searching every café and asking at every hotel. 'Tall Englishman, charming smile.' The descriptions lead nowhere. It is as if he's vanished into thin air, taking my heart and savings with him.

I check my bank account again; the numbers haven't changed. The thirty thousand pounds I transferred is still gone, just like James.

How have I gotten here? How have I, Jane Steele, a sensible fifty-five-year-old woman with a successful career, grown children, and grandchildren, ended up alone in Cyprus, hunting a ghost?

It started, as these things often do, with a smile...

Chapter One – Divorce

'Gavin, we need to talk,' I snap, my voice a controlled fury barely containing the chaos churning in my gut.

My husband of the last twenty-four and a half years stands in front of me, arms crossed and eyes blazing.

'Talk? Well, that's a novelty. You're usually too consumed with yourself and the kids to notice, much less talk to me.'

'That's completely unfair!' I shoot back. I usually avoid confrontation at all costs, but this time, frustration boils over. 'I've been here for you! I thought we were both parents to our children, not just me!'

He shakes his head, a smirk twisting his lips. 'Yeah? You left me feeling neglected and unloved, so you can't complain that I found comfort elsewhere.'

My heart races. How dare he? Each word feels like a punch to my stomach. I swallow hard, struggling to contain the anger boiling within me.

'We have a busy life! I have work, the kids, and this house to manage, because you are never here. I'm exhausted! I can't greet you at the door in a negligée every time you choose to stumble in and pay your family a visit! But does that really justify what you did? Let me tell you, it doesn't, because... You betrayed me when I was doing my best!'

Gavin steps back, eyeing me coldly, which stokes the fire within me. 'I don't owe you an explanation. I did what I had to do, so playing the victim won't work this time,' he spits, his tone laced with disdain, as without any hesitation, he pulls a bag from the wardrobe and flings it on the bed before me.

It feels like he is enjoying my humiliation as I watch him helplessly; each item he slides into his bag feels like a physical blow. My fingers dig into my palms, my nails leave crescent marks on my skin, and the room spins as I struggle to breathe through the tightness in my chest. A muscle jumps in my jaw as I clench my teeth to prevent myself from screaming words I can't take back.

'Gavin, please,' I hiss, my voice trembling with rage and desperation. But he ignores me, refusing to meet my gaze. Instead, he strides toward the door with a swagger that infuriates me further.

The heavy thud of his footsteps echoes down the stairs, each step a brutal reminder of the love he so easily tossed aside. I want to scream, to throw something at him, but I stand frozen as the front door slams shut, echoing through the house like a gunshot. His car roars to life, and my mind races – where is he going? To her, I think bitterly. He's like an animal, and I have set him loose to chase after someone new.

I take a shaky breath and try to quell the nausea churning within me as a single tear drifts down my cheek, an unspoken farewell to everything we were. 'It's over,' I whisper into the stillness. My heart aches for civility and closure. But deep down, I know I'm left with an invisible scar, a haunting reminder of the love we once shared and the dreams we built together, which are now shattered.

The struggle for closure is ongoing and energy-sapping, an uphill battle I'm not sure I'm strong enough to fight. Gavin made the call to a divorce lawyer the day that he left, and the papers lay on the kitchen table like a weight pressing down on my chest – a stark representation of a past I wish I could rewrite. Each glance at them tugs at my heart, and I'm left clutching the fragments of what might have been. I yearn so deeply for this story to have a different ending.

Chapter Two – Getting Back Out There

As I rebuild my life after Divorce, my children embark on their university paths, and I miss the chaos of family life. I married young and have never lived alone before. No matter how much time I spend at work, the gym, running, or out with friends, I always have to go home to my ever-present housemate: Loneliness.

I may be lonely, but as I stand before my new full-length mirror, I meet the gaze of a woman with a soft glow to her skin, a relatively fit-toned body, and a reflection that smiles back at me with a subtle hint of allure.

'I don't look my age,' I reflect, allowing a flicker of pride to stir.

I admit to being a hopeless romantic, convinced that love is out there. Comparing myself to a butterfly egg, I am just waiting to find love and confidence to help me metamorphose into a vibrant beauty, a woman who exudes warmth and fun – but I also admit to finding the idea of a romantic connection both exhilarating and daunting.

'I may not be ready yet, but how will I ever know if I don't take the leap?' I whisper to my reflection, my voice trembling with longing and uncertainty. Each word carries the weight of my dreams, echoing in the silent room, challenging me to embrace the unknown.

Stepping into the realm of being a naive single woman searching for love feels like teetering on the edge of an uncharted ocean. A chance encounter with a man at the café sends me reeling. When he flashes that disarming smile, my stomach twists into an exhilarating knot – is it flirtation or mere friendliness? Ambiguity sweeps over me like a tidal wave, and I find myself fleeing from his gaze, desperately focusing on anything but him. And to add to my embarrassment, red heat rushes to my cheeks as my breath quickens, caught in the whirlwind of my own inexperience.

'Just breathe,' I remind myself, but the anxiety lingers like a heavy cloak. My innate shyness feels like an anchor, dragging down any budding connection. Just yesterday, at Sainsbury's, I was fumbling with my trolley when a nice-looking man caught my eye.

'Hi,' he said, and my response – a weak, squeaky 'Hello' – left me feeling so pathetic. It stings the way that my confidence, as well as my voice, betrays me, turning me invisible.

Every compliment feels like a test – my throat tightens, and words are swallowed into silence. The fear of not being enough swells inside me, almost tangible, and I can't help but wonder: Will I ever be brave enough to step into the light and claim what could be mine?

'Come on, there's a lid for every pot,' my oldest friend, Susan, reminds me. Her tone is warm and encouraging, and ignites a flicker of hope. I laugh as I share my vision of a lid wandering the world, just like I am – searching for that perfect fit, waiting for the moment it finds me.

As I turn back to my reflection, a wave of determination washes over me. 'I may not be as youthful as I once was,' I whisper, acknowledging the truth in my heart, 'but the possibility of love keeps my spirit alive.' Each day feels like a gentle invitation into the unknown. 'I will keep searching,' I promise myself, allowing my heart to remain open to whatever lies ahead, ready to embrace the journey with all its uncertainties.

Online Dating

The soft glow of my laptop screen warms the small table, casting playful shadows that dance against the walls. I take a deep breath, my fingers poised above the keyboard, as memories of the last time I was part of the dating world – nearly thirty years ago – swirl in my mind like leaves caught in a restless autumn breeze.

'It's been five years since everything shattered,' I whisper, the echoes of betrayals and unrealised dreams still raw. The memory of Gavin's deceit and the dream of the happy ever after he snatched away still haunt me. Old conversations replay in my head, but now I find myself teetering on the edge of a new chapter, one that I finally get to write for myself.

Fidgeting with the leather strap of my wristwatch, I feel its smoothness as I contemplate my task. An online profile – just the thought sends a rush of adrenaline through me. I envision a vibrant photograph that captures my smile, a perfect blend of resilience and authenticity etched in every line of my face.

'What do I want them to see?' I muse aloud, my mind racing with possibilities. 'Kitchen Goddess, Spontaneous Adventurer? Or a normal girl who loves nothing better than a great book and an even better cup of coffee?' Each thought paints a brushstroke on a blank canvas waiting to be filled.

A wave of uncertainty washes over me, and I pause. 'Will my vulnerabilities shine through?' I ponder, biting my lip, wrestling with the polished facade I feel tempted to craft. But then, I remind myself of the courage it takes to be vulnerable and feel a surge of inspiration.

With a mix of hope and trepidation, I lean in. My fingers hover above the keys; I will create a testament of who I am now and who I aspire to be in this brave new world of mid-life dating, where fakes, fraudsters, and possibly axe murderers could hide behind a lovely smile. But as I start typing, words spill forth, weaving together a narrative that brings me closer to revealing my true self.

'I need to find the right man this time,' I remind myself, carefully selecting each word. There is no room for players or liars. 'This isn't just a profile,' I affirm, feeling a sense of empowerment. 'It's a beacon calling out to someone else lost in the fog of mid-life dating, yearning for connection.' I scroll through my revisions, the weight of each choice pressing down on me. 'Fun, loyal, kind and honest,' I whisper, 'that's what I want to shine through.'

A satisfied smile creeps onto my face, and my heart races with newfound purpose. 'Now for a profile picture!' I declare as I dive into my phone gallery. Images from the past flash by, but none resonate with the reflection in the mirror of the woman I am today.

'Nothing feels fresh,' I huff, determination surging. Grabbing my phone, I set it up in front of me. 'Alright, let's do this.' I adjust the angles to capture the best light in my cosy living room, discomfort bubbling within me at the thought of the whole 'shop window' scenario, where I can't help feeling that I am advertising my heart.

'Just breathe,' I remind myself as I peer into the screen of my phone.

A 'click' reveals a study of a vibrant fifty-five-year-old woman who is full of life yet feels lighter than ever and ready to embrace her next chapter.

Chapter Three – Finding Love

My diligence in creating the online dating profile has paid off. It has brought James Warner into my life. A warm glow fills me as I sit here, basking in the joy of meeting him. James, a successful engineer with a passion for adventure and luxury, has a way of making me feel special.

James has the most captivating smile that weakens my knees. He is everything I've ever dreamed of and then some. I've tossed caution and inhibitions aside and feel like I'm living in a whirlwind romance straight out of a Danielle Steel novel. His passionate declarations of love envelop me in a thrilling adventure, and I can't get enough of his dazzling attention!

My phone buzzes, and I glance at the screen – and my heart skips a beat.

'Hey, beautiful! Are you up for a walk on the beach?'

I beam with excitement as I respond, 'Always. Meet you in ten?' The anticipation of seeing him fills me with joy.

The evening air, cool and refreshing, brushes against my skin as I leave, and the horizon glows vibrant orange. James is waiting, a vision of Ralph Lauren man, with his tall, athletic frame silhouetted against the setting sun. Our eyes meet, and

I skip across the crisp gravel of the car park and into his arms, and once I'm there, the world around us fades.

'It's been a whole day since we have seen each other. Did you miss me?' he teases, a playful smirk dancing on his lips.

'Of course I did,' I reply, nudging him gently.

We stroll along the beach, the sand cool beneath our feet. Our laughter blends with the sound of the waves.

'I can't remember the last time I felt this alive,' I admit, glancing up at him. And I also can't believe I am here with someone so handsome, but I keep that comment to myself.

He locks eyes with me, a playful sparkle igniting an exhilarating flutter deep inside, as if nurturing those butterfly eggs within me into their transformative rebirth.

'Neither can I,' he says, his voice warm and inviting. 'You have a way of making everything feel so much brighter.'

As the sun dips lower, we find ourselves at our favourite harbourside bar, sharing grilled shrimp and sipping cold wine. His hand brushes against mine, and it's electric.

'Are you coming back with me tonight?' I ask with a hint of mischief in my voice.

'Definitely,' he replies, his gaze intense, sparking a thrill down my spine.

There's something extraordinary about our connection – it's brimming with passion and excitement. Yet, there is a wall that James has built around his past and certain parts of his present that unnerves me. As I attempt to peel back the layers and truly understand the mystery that is him, he skilfully sidesteps my probing questions, and in my eagerness to please and hold onto this incredible man, I find myself letting those moments slide.

James is an experienced lover, and I am completely addicted to the way that he makes me feel. Our nights are passionate and intense, and I watch him with a mix of admiration and longing every morning as he dresses for the day. His designer jeans and T-shirt hug his athletic frame, showcasing his style and confidence. He knows how sexy he is and pauses at the door, glancing back at me, also knowing that I have so many unanswered questions. In that moment, the air is thick with unspoken promises. 'One day, I'll tell you everything about me and my work,' he murmurs, his voice smooth and earnest, leaving me aching for that day to arrive.

After only a month together, life with James feels like a beautiful, intoxicating dream overflowing with love, passion and endless possibilities.

The Business Trip

James sits cross-legged on the plush sofa of the Hyatt Hotel's Penthouse suite, his laptop glowing like a beacon in the dim light. The rhythmic tapping of keys fills the air, a soft melody against the tranquil yet charged atmosphere. I glance over at him, intrigued by the focus etched on his brow and the slight smile that dances on his lips as he types.

'Hey,' I break the quiet spell, curiosity bubbling. 'What's got you so engrossed?'

He looks up and hastily closes the laptop, as if uncomfortable with my interest. 'I'm just finalising some plans for the trip. New York is mostly about tying up loose ends, but the project in Istanbul?' He leans forward, eyes sparkling. 'It's incredible.'

A bittersweet tug pulls at my heartstrings.

'Two weeks without you feels like an eternity.'

He chuckles softly, running a hand through his tousled hair. The warmth of his laughter sends a ripple of comfort through me. 'It's not that long. I'll be back before you know it, and then you will have my undivided attention.' His words envelop me like a reassuring hug, easing the ache in my heart.

Our night before the trip is filled with passion, plans and declarations of forever, but it's over all too quickly, and before I know it, it's time for him to leave.

I stand here outside the airport in his arms as I inhale deeply, enjoying the lingering scent of his expensive aftershave, a vivid reminder of our night together. 'I will treasure memories of last night,' I whisper, a hint of nostalgia colouring my voice.

'So will I,' he replies, his gaze drawing me further into the moment. 'Last night was... special.'

My mind drifts back to the warmth of our farewell lovemaking, the electric thrill of his skin against my lips, and I swallow hard, letting those memories wash over me.

'Okay, enough with the sentimentality,' he says, a playful grin breaking through. 'I must dash; my flight won't wait for me.'

Despite my smile, I feel a tightness in my chest as we walk hand in hand toward the airport's departure hall. Heathrow Airport buzzes with activity, but I can only focus on James.

'Just one more hug?' I implore, my voice barely above a whisper, the vulnerability in my words hanging in the air.

He chuckles gently, his eyes sparkling. 'I can't deny you that.' He pulls me close, wrapping his arms around me, and our hearts beat in perfect harmony for a fleeting moment.

'And one last kiss...' I murmur as our lips meet, and the chaos around us fades away, leaving just the two of us wrapped in a cocoon of warmth.

James pulls away, his brow furrowed with determination, an undeniable magnetism radiating from him. 'I really have to go,' he says, glancing back over his shoulder.

'Be safe,' I urge, searching his gaze for a glimmer of reassurance, a lifeline in the uncertainty.

In response, he breaks into a broad smile, his confidence lighting up the space between us. 'I love you!' he calls out, each word echoing with promise as he strides through the door, leaving me standing there, filled with love and a longing that feels as vast as the distance that will soon be stretching between us.

A week rushes by in a blur of anticipation. My phone buzzes nonstop with James's messages, each crackling with energy and excitement. 'Meetings were incredible!' 'You wouldn't believe the vibe here!' he texts, his enthusiasm infectious and igniting a spark in me with every ping. But when he calls, I think that I catch the slight cracks in his exuberant tone.

'Hey, beautiful!' he greets, but I sense what I assume is the weight of travel fatigue beneath his words. The line crackles, and I can almost picture him pacing through the bustling JFK airport, his hair a glorious mess from running his hand through it in frustration and excitement.

'I'm finally done in New York and heading to the plane for Istanbul! I can't wait to dive into that city!' His voice shines enthusiastically, yet the late nights and early mornings lurk in the background, a reminder of what he explains is the jet lag chasing him.

'I wish I were there with you,' I reply, my heart racing at the thought of being swept away in the thrill of it all.

'Oh, you'd love it! The energy in Istanbul is just... electric!' He falters for a moment, breath shaky and almost overwhelmed. 'I miss you. It's not the same without you by my side.'

The distance between us feels like a yawning chasm, but I hold onto the joy sparkling in his words. 'Just think of all the stories we'll share when you're back,' I encourage softly, my voice a quiet tether to him, filled with the belief in our shared future.

'Yeah,' he chuckles, and I can almost envision his grin cutting through the chaos around him. 'And I've brought you something very special in New York, let's just say ...I want the world to know that you are mine!'

I close my eyes, picturing him picking out a huge diamond for me to wear on my engagement finger, blown away by the promise of my future with this man. 'Be safe, okay, I'll eagerly await your call once you land in Turkey!' I say, and the line goes quiet.

As I sit in the stillness, a whirlwind of emotions churns inside me – the ache of missing James and the thrill of knowing we're on this wild ride together, even with oceans crashing between us. The love that is alive in our hearts is enough to keep my spirit soaring.

Over and Out From Istanbul

James usually spends hours chatting with me on the phone, but since arriving in Istanbul, he has felt slightly off. 'How are things going?' I ask, hoping to reconnect.

'It's fine,' he says, his tone lacking energy. 'Just... you know, different.'

'Different, how?' I press, sensing there's more beneath the surface.

He shrugs. ' It's just not as... easy here as I thought,' he replies vaguely, his voice devoid of warmth.

I sigh, yearning for clarity but feeling like I'm getting nowhere. 'I miss our talks.'

'Yeah, me too. But things change,' he eventually replies.

I take a figurative step closer, carefully assessing the moment's weight. 'Are you okay? You seem...' I pause, searching for the right words, my concern deepening. '...lost.'

James sighs heavily, and I can feel the depth of his vulnerability: 'I don't know. Maybe I am lost. Everything here feels very wrong.'

The distance between us seems unbridgeable now, and my heart aches for my friend, the man I've fallen in love with, who has always been so confident, so full of laughter and stories. 'I'm here for you, you know. Whenever you want to talk.'

'Thanks, I appreciate it,' he responds, but the gratitude feels overshadowed by despair. It's as if we're both caught in quicksand, and I'm desperately trying to reach out to a man who seems to be sinking deeper with every moment that passes.

Ten days, each one heavier than the last, filled with his suffocating silences, drag on. I run my fingers over my stomach, where confusion and frustration knots tighten. Today, though, I can't hold back any longer.

With a deep breath, I confront him. 'James, what's going on? You're keeping secrets from me.'

I catch a flicker in his voice – fear? Guilt? 'I need you to trust me,' he says, his voice barely a whisper, almost too soft.

'I want to trust you,' I respond, my heart racing. 'But every time I reach out, you push me away. What are you hiding?'

He shifts his tone, agitation evident. 'You know my business is highly confidential and complex,' he says, this stock response making my skin crawl. 'I promise I'll explain everything when I get home. Please, give me a little more time.'

However, something about his plea feels off – a veil of unease shrouds his words. I can't shake the feeling that something sinister is buried beneath the surface.

The weight of his secrets hangs heavily in the air, suffocating any glimmer of hope. The ache in my chest grows sharper, a relentless mix of despair, love, and an overwhelming sense of doubt. 'How long do I have to hold on?' I whisper, but the following silence offers no comfort, only emptiness.

Days stretch endlessly before me, and loneliness has returned as my companion, but this time it is overwhelming; the distance between calls with James is a chasm that feels impassable. We are trapped in this suffocating silence, and the shadows of unspoken words loom larger, a reminder of the rift that seems impossible to bridge. But today, as I sense the air thickening with tension, I hear James take a deep, steadying breath. I know him, and I can almost visualise how his body tenses, every muscle coiling in anticipation before he finds the courage to speak. 'I can't keep this inside anymore,' he says, his voice trembling as if on the verge of breaking like a fragile dam.

At that moment, a loud bang echoes through the room, and I imagine him slamming his fist on the table, causing the cups to rattle and the atmosphere to shift. 'They seized my passport. My taxes... I've messed up, and they're unpaid.'

A wave of disbelief washes over me, swiftly followed by a deep surge of compassion that fades my irritation into the background. I can feel the weight of his predicament, the fear and shame that must consume him. 'But surely that can be resolved,' I gently encourage. 'You have the money, so why don't you take care of what you owe?'

What follows is like a gathering storm cloud, each revelation deepening the shadow of his desperation. 'I was holding out to earn more interest on the money, and now...' he pauses, his voice hitching as he continues, 'I can't access my bank account. My bank has frozen my online banking, and they say I need to visit them in Zurich to reset it. However, I obviously can't do that without my passport. I am so, so sorry, Jane. I've messed up,' he cries, his anguish palpable and heartbreaking. I can feel the depth of his regret, and it breaks my heart.

At this moment, I only want to offer him comfort and understanding, to let him know he isn't alone. A waterfall of determination washes through me. 'How much do you owe?' I respond tentatively, my stomach twisting with anticipation.

'£50,000,' James snaps back, his tone sharp and unyielding, leaving me reeling. The weight of the number hangs in the air between us, heavier than I could have ever imagined.

From that moment, every question I pose feels like I'm speaking through glass, my voice muffled by an invisible 'Confidential' barrier surrounding his business. I sense the walls closing in. I'm standing at a crossroads, wrestling with my feelings. My heart pulls me towards him, craving the intimacy of connection, the comfort of love, and the promise of unwavering loyalty. But my mind is a whirlwind of doubt, echoing warnings about the risks of being entwined in a web of secrecy. The thought of walking away teeters on the edge of my consciousness, tempting me with visions of clarity and freedom. I feel torn, each emotion pulling me in conflicting directions, anchoring me to a vital and terrifying decision.

It's been days since we last spoke, and I'm drowning in swirling emotions and unanswered questions when at last my phone buzzes.

'Hey, it's me!' Given the storm brewing inside me, James's voice is bright and infused with an almost comical enthusiasm.

'Hi,' I reply, my brain processing the absurdity of his cheerful tone. How dare he play with my emotions like this? Is he some master illusionist? Yet, despite my irritation, my heart inexplicably skips a beat at the sound of his voice.

'I just want to remind you of what we share,' he continues, his tone so playful it's as if he's talking about a game instead of our complicated feelings. 'You know, all those moments –'

'Yeah, I remember,' I say, a smile breaking through my frustration, which feels like the ultimate irony – finding joy in a tangled mess.

'It's special, isn't it?' he asks, wrapping me in a bubble of hope that feels more like a balloon ready to pop.

'Yeah, it really is,' I confess, my heart doing a little jig amidst the chaos of my mind. 'But you still hold back,' I say, sarcasm creeping in like a friendly intruder. 'Why can't you just open up to me?'

'It's not that simple,' he replies, his voice now tight, and I can't help but wonder if he's perpetually three steps behind in this twisted dance. 'You don't understand the stakes,' he says, a tremor of desperation lacing his voice. 'But don't forget I have ten million dollars waiting for us in Switzerland.' The gravity of his words hangs heavy between us, both a promise and a threat.

I close my eyes momentarily, trying to grasp the magnitude of what he's saying. Images flood my mind – his proud grin when he revealed his Swiss Bank account statement just before his departure. 'I have the means to give you a wonderful future; you just need to trust me and believe in us.' Those words echo, but now they feel like whispers from a stranger.

There's a tension in the air, thick like the fog rolling in from the sea. 'You've changed since you arrived in Turkey,' I say, my voice barely above a whisper. 'You were so loving, so full of life. It feels like you're drifting away.'

'I am not a robot,' he snaps, his frustration evident. 'I can only respond to how I feel.' It's clear that everything has spiralled beyond our control, and I can feel my heart racing in response to the rising conflict. 'A little understanding instead of endless questions would be nice,' he adds.

His sarcasm catches me off guard and breaks my heart as I struggle to find the right words. 'I'm sorry,' I finally say, my voice trembling. 'But I love you; all I want is to help.' The pain of imagining his struggle grips me, and I can't bear it. 'Please James, let me in.'

Chapter Four – What's Mine is Yours, and What's Yours is Mine

I sit at my kitchen table, fingers trembling over the mouse, haunted by what may lie ahead. The dull hum of the laptop's fan fills the room, a monotonous backdrop to the rhythm of raindrops tapping against the window like a relentless drum of sorrow.

With a deep sigh, I click the 'send' button, and it feels like a part of me disappears with my hard-earned £5000 of savings. Initially, there's a fleeting relief – £45,000 left to go (which I believe that James should be able to raise from his business associates) – and a brief escape from the suffocating pressure of indecision. But that moment is quickly swallowed by an overwhelming tide of panic; the potential implications of what many might call a reckless impulse to bring James home drag me into an abyss of uncertainty. Each passing second feels heavier, as if the weight of possible failure pulls me deeper into a void from which there is no escape.

It's agonisingly two days later when my phone buzzes, and James's voice bursts through with brightness and gratitude.

'Thank you, my love! The money's arrived!' he exclaims, his joy almost radiating through the line. I can easily picture his wide smile, even from miles away.

'That's great!' I reply, trying to match his excitement.

'You've done the right thing. We're going to get through this,' James reassures me, his words embracing me. There's a slight tremor in his voice, but it only adds to the sincerity of his reassurance. His words are a balm to my worried mind.

'I hope so,' I respond, feeling a flicker of optimism in my chest. We chat and share stories like the old days, with laughter and flirty giggles cutting through the heaviness that had settled on our love. Though an eerie silence falls over the room when the call ends, I can still feel the warmth of our conversation lingering in the air. I sit back, a newfound courage swelling within me, and focus on the promise of brighter days ahead.

As the week drags on, once again, I can feel the tension between us thickening. James's excitement is fading, and a tone of desperation hangs heavily in his voice. 'Alex and I are working so hard, but it's not enough. We have only managed to raise £20,000, which still leaves us £25,000 short,' he says, each word dripping with disappointment that settles like a stone in my stomach. My doubts simmer beneath the surface, threatening to boil over. I can feel the weight of what I now consider 'our' financial struggles press down on me, a constant reminder of our precarious situation.

Then, as if he's testing the very limits of our bond, James ambushes me, his voice pleading. 'Do you love me enough to borrow £25,000 for me?'

The question hangs there, charged and oppressive, suffocating the space between us. A wave of nausea rolls through me, and I grip the fabric of my sweater, scrambling for the right words amid the chaos swirling in my mind. My heart races, and I can feel the sweat beading on my forehead, a physical manifestation of my emotional turmoil.

'I've just repaid all my debts, James,' I manage to whisper, my voice trembling. 'And I've taken on a mortgage for this house. Getting another loan... I don't think I can do that.' I can feel the shadow of his disappointment creeping in, chilling me to the bone, and his silence is unbearable, stretching like a taut wire ready to snap. 'I just... don't want you to think I don't trust you,' I say weakly, but my words fall flat against the weight of our dilemma.

'Well, you obviously don't trust me or love me,' James responds aggressively. His accusation is like a dark cloud. And I realise with a sinking feeling how quickly love can warp into heartbreak, and how easily James's anger can coil around us like a noose, tightening and threatening to strangle everything that once was so perfect.

A small, stuffy office in Istanbul

James's fingers drum a restless beat against the wobbly table's edge. He is agitated, his gaze fixed on the phone; the dim light of the office flickers, casting shadows that seem to mock his unease. 'Come on, Jane,' he mutters through gritted teeth, frustration bubbling beneath the surface.

Alex Leo reclines against the padding of his faux leather executive chair, his grey fake designer suit – a sharp imitation of Armani – gleaming under the flickering fluorescent light. The shabby office around him feels like a world apart, an ecosystem of dust and disarray where, on the surface, he stands out like a peacock.

With a casual flick of his wrist, he adjusts the cuff of his shirt, the iridescent teal fabric catching the light just so. A smirk curls at the corners of his mouth as he watches James shift nervously in the dim room, wiping his palms on the thick denim of his jeans. Every uneasy movement that James makes echoes louder than a bell tolling.

Alex crosses his arms, settling deeper into the upholstery and favouring the way it cradles him. He leans forward slightly, his gaze steady and piercing, the corners of his eyes crinkling just enough to signal amusement. Each bead of sweat that trickles down James's temple seems to fuel Alex's delight, reinforcing the power dynamic at play. This is his stage, and he revels in the performance. "You look like you're about to leap out of your skin. Everything alright?"

James rubs the back of his neck, the angry red mark betraying the calm he tries to project. 'Yeah, I'm just... waiting for news from Jane. She was supposed to call about the loan.' His breath comes out in a rush, laced with impatience.

'Are you losing your touch, mate?' Alex says, leaning forward. The sarcasm in his tone sits heavily in the room's stale air. 'You thought that she seemed very resourceful.'

James shakes his head violently, tightening his lips, betraying his thoughts. 'Resourceful? More like she's reaching her limit with my problems. What if she doesn't care enough to fight for us? I may have pushed her too far.'

Silence falls on the room, each tick of the clock amplifying the anxiety that twists in James's gut. He needs that money! His eyes are glued to the phone, as if compelling it to ring through sheer willpower.

Suddenly, the top-of-the-range iPhone, its shiny platinum casing looking out of place as it is balanced on the dusty table, bursts into life, shattering the tension. James jumps, and Alex's eyes sparkle with a predatory glint, a mix of expectation and calculated intrigue. 'Lucky boy!' He smirks, nodding toward the device as if it were a trophy.

James stands, pacing the small room, his footsteps frantic. 'Hello, beautiful,' he says into the phone, but as the conversation unfolds, his expression twists into a mask of frustration. His voice cracks angrily, and Alex catches snippets of an argument that seems to escalate.

As James's face contorts under the weight of bad news, Alex revels in the unfolding drama. Watching his associate navigate this storm is a spectacle, but he steels himself for the role he knows he has to play. With the right words and an emotive incentive, he can mould the situation to his favour, knowing that his trump card is third-party emotional manipulation, and he is very good at that.

My phone vibrates gently. The shadowy glow of an unfamiliar Turkish number illuminates the room. I freeze for a moment, my heart drumming against my chest like a small bird trying to escape. The decision to answer or not feels like a heavyweight one. Steeling myself, I swipe to answer, inhaling deeply to calm my nerves.

'Hello?' I say, attempting to project confidence, though my voice trembles slightly.

'Good afternoon, Jane. This is Alex Leo, James's solicitor in Istanbul,' comes a smooth, velvety voice, rich with a Mediterranean lilt that quickens my pulse.

'James's solicitor?' I echo, my mind racing as thoughts tumble over each other. 'What's going on?'

'Rest assured, everything is under control,' he assures me, his tone somehow soothing despite the weight of his words. 'I just need you to realise how vital your support is in this matter. After all, you are his future wife.'

I pause, a rush of warmth flooding me at the thought of James's commitment. It's as if he had whispered sweet promises in my ear moments before. 'What do you need me to do?' I ask.

'We need your assistance to settle a tax bill that is holding everything up,' Alex explains, his words dripping with urgency and a hint of charm. 'If you could take out a loan on his behalf, it would change everything. Your involvement will not only help him but also demonstrate your true devotion.'

His voice is like a siren song, wrapping around my mind and heart, urging me to step forward. 'I'm here to guide you through this process,' he continues, his words weaving a narrative of hope and stability, each one a persuasive stroke on the canvas of my emotions. 'Together, we can bring this matter to a swift conclusion.'

'But I thought you and he would have the rest of the money covered. James told me he has contacts!' I resist weakly.

'Sadly, our associates cannot help us with the full amount outstanding on this occasion. I believe that James has already advised you that we can only raise £20,000 from them,' Alex replies firmly.

As we converse, each word feels like a thread binding me closer to James, and with each passing moment, determination blossoms within me. When I finally hang up, I realise that I'm not just a bystander in this; I'm a crucial player in a story that promises love and a shared future. My role is not just significant, it's indispensable.

My mind is a whirlwind as I sink into my favourite spot on the couch, grappling with a potent mix of unease and hope from James's solicitor's call. But what lurks beneath this glimmer? 'What if he's not who I think he is?' I whisper, and the thought sends a shiver down my spine. And so, with a leaden heart, I open my laptop, fingers trembling with anticipation, ready to plunge into a sea of information I should have deciphered long ago.

'Come on, just a bit of clarity; who are you, James? Who is Alex Leo? What am I being asked to get into, and what is your business really about?' I mutter, scrolling through endless articles, each tugging my frustration further. Each click feels like a step deeper into a void, the silence around them echoing louder – good news or alarm bells ringing, I can't tell. Uncertainty and fear that I am somehow being lured into something that I don't understand keep me on edge, and is a constant weight on my shoulders, a cloud over my thoughts, a knot in my stomach that refuses to untie.

Yet, as I stumble upon stories about Turkey's political instability, the knot tightens, and I stare intently at the screen, the gravity of it all weighing heavily on me. 'James... how did you end up intertwined with all this?' I murmur, picturing him far away, perhaps ensnared in a web of corruption, alone and vulnerable. My heart aches, love sweeps over me even as confusion muddles my mind. I know that secrets lie beneath the surface of his life, but befriending Google has failed to uncover anything negative about James Warner or Alex Leo.

So, the decision, heavy with implications, is made, and consequently, here I am, at the kitchen table, nerves fraying as an email offering to lend me £25000 fills my laptop screen.

'I can't believe I'm doing this,' I mutter, biting down hard on my lip as I meticulously scroll through the fine print for what feels like the hundredth time. The interest rate is high and hangs over me, yet another suffocating weight, but it will only be for a month or so, and then James will repay it. I take a deep breath, trying to catch a whiff of the comforting coffee aroma, but it feels distant, almost mocking. Images of a future with James crowd my mind – sunsets, laughter, and shared dreams – each one a reminder of what hangs in the balance.

'Am I sure about this?' I ask the stillness, but the silence is only broken by the relentless thrum of my heartbeat, drowning out the click as I e-sign the document and accept the loan.

I start the process of transferring the outstanding money to James. Ultimately, this will allow him to embark on a journey from Istanbul to the central tax office in Ankara, where he will settle his tax bill, retrieve his passport, and then fly to Zurich to sort out his bank account before returning home to me forever. Well, that's the plan, anyway.

James's Story – Ankara

James ducks into the shade of a crumbling stone wall as the relentless sun beats down on Ankara, casting a vibrant golden glow over the ancient city. Sweat trickles down his brow, and he squints against the glaring light. 'Are you ready for this?' he asks, glancing at Alex, who bounces on his heels, a mix of excitement and nerves coursing through him.

Alex nods, gripping a sleek brown case tightly against his chest, the weight of its secrets heavy in the air. 'Absolutely. Let's do this.'

'Just remember, it's just for the paperwork and to settle their ridiculous tax demands,' James says, attempting to inject more confidence into his voice. The large cheque feels like a boulder in his pocket, a stark reminder of their mission's risks.

'Yes! Paperwork that can change everything!' Alex replies, his enthusiasm momentarily overshadowing his anxiety. 'And it's a nice bonus for me!'

James gives Alex an encouraging pat on the shoulder. 'Perfect! It's a win-win for both of us! Now, let's get in there and wrap this up.'

Taking a deep breath, Alex tightens his grip on the case, steeling himself for what lies ahead. Together, they push toward the imposing government building ahead.

'Can you believe this heat?' Alex huffs, adjusting his shirt, which clings like a second skin. 'We're going to melt before we even make it inside.'

James scans the bustling street, the chaotic blur of people around them. 'Keep your wits about you. Did you see that man by the café? I have a bad feeling – like we're being watched.'

'Yeah, I noticed him!' Alex whispers, stealing glances behind them. 'Let's not stick around to find out if we're right. We need to move.'

With a sharp intake of breath, James pushes forward, the dry dust swirling beneath their hurried steps. 'Stick close. If we stay low-profile, they won't clock us,' he instructs, adrenaline sparking within him.

'Right,' Alex replies, mimicking James's pace. 'Act casual.'

'Casual? I feel anything but!' James quips, trying to catch his breath as they navigate through the throng of bodies. Anxiety twists in his gut as they hasten their steps and divert into a maze of passageways as eerie shadows lengthen around them.

Suddenly, James's voice drops to a whisper. 'What if they're playing games with us? What if they don't return my passport?' He leans in closer, intensity sharpening his tone. 'Do you think they'll follow the rules?' He rakes a hand through his hair, a nervous habit surfacing.

Alex crosses his arms protectively around the briefcase, scanning the narrow path ahead. 'I think so,' he replies, steel creeping into his gaze. 'I double-checked with my contacts; everything checks out. I wouldn't have brought you here if I thought it was a setup.'

Panic flickers across James's face, his fists clenching tightly. 'I can't be stuck here forever. What's the plan if things go south? We can't let them take us down!'

Alex takes a deep breath, feeling the tension bouncing around their claustrophobic surroundings. 'If they try anything, we run. We need to be one step ahead.'

James exhales shakily, the uncertainty gnawing at him. 'But what if –'

Before he can finish, Alex's phone buzzes violently in his pocket. He pulls it out, his face paling as he reads the text. 'James, it's bad. We can't go in there – it's a trap. They're waiting to arrest you.'

Staggering back, James feels his breath quicken, panic overtaking him. 'What? Why? What's happening?'

'Charges – attempted coup,' Alex urges, urgency flooding his voice. 'They have proof you met with General Aslan. They believe you were involved in his conspiracy to overthrow the government.' His eyes dart around as he points at the email, disbelief washing over them. 'This tax issue is bait to draw you in; they think you're a traitor.'

'What?' James blurts out, incredulity written all over his face. 'This is madness! I only met with him for the engineering contract – nothing more!' His fists clench again as he fights to grasp the gravity of the situation.

The clamorous noise of the city buzzes around them, but inside the narrow passage, silence hangs thick like fog. 'We can't just run! That passport is everything!'

'James!' Alex's voice cuts through the chaos, firm and resolute, as he grabs James by the shoulder. 'We don't have a choice. We need to be out of here – now.'

Taking a shaky breath, James feels his heart thumping in his chest like a war drum. 'But... where do we go?'

'Trust me,' Alex replies, scanning the shadows before gesturing toward a darkened route that leads deeper into the seedier side of Ankara. 'There's a safe house nearby. We can regroup there and plan our next move.'

With reluctance, James nods, allowing Alex to tug him into the shadows. The city sounds fade behind them, replaced by the rhythm of their urgent footsteps echoing off the stone walls. Anxiety prickles at James's skin, but he focuses on keeping pace with Alex. 'So, they are indeed watching us?'

'We'll be fine,' Alex assures, glancing ahead cautiously. 'Just keep moving. They can't track what they can't see.'

The two men break into a sprint, shadows flitting past as the stakes of their mission soar higher. James pushes forward, his mind racing with possibilities, each stride of his long legs drawing him closer to the unknown but away from danger.

The clock ticks softly, its rhythmic sound contrasting sharply with the shadows that embrace the room, deepening the silence that feels almost suffocating. When my phone buzzes, it pierces through the stillness, and my heart races in response. I sit up abruptly, my eyes drawn to the screen – James's name shines back at me, a very welcome beacon in the darkness. As I swipe to read the message, a moment of anticipation sparks, only to be quelled by an overwhelming wave of sorrow as his tale unravels.

'No, no, no...' I whisper, my voice barely breaking the stillness. As the lengthy text unveiling James's story unfolds, a lump forms in my throat, constricting my breath. My fingers tremble around the phone; its coldness stokes turmoil inside me. It feels as though the room has become a heavy shroud, each corner steeped in silence that mirrors my despair. My heart, a wild animal, beats against my ribs, desperate for escape.

Pulling my knees close, I wrap my arms around them, as if seeking refuge from the reality that weighs heavily on my chest. 'Why?' I breathe out, the question a painful echo in my mind, each inhalation growing more shallow and uneven. Tears begin to spill uncontrollably, soaking the pillow beneath me, the fabric bearing silent witness to my spiralling grief.

Time stretches, the tick of the clock amplifying the disbelief that constricts my heart. 'I can't... I can't believe this.

What have you got me mixed up in, James? I have sent you money; I am an accomplice. If they were watching you, James, are they now watching me?' I choke out, burying my face in the duvet, feeling as though I'm suffocating beneath the weight of his words, desperately wishing I could erase them from my existence. I wish I could pause the world if only to escape the pain and fear raging through me, even if it is just for a moment.

Chapter Five - Cyprus or Bust

It's been a long five months waiting for the dust to settle. Intelligence sources have confirmed that James is no longer actively being searched for by the authorities, so it is hoped that a fake ID will be sufficient to get him through the various checkpoints en route and ultimately across the Turkish border.

As I listen to James speak passionately about his dreams of being home with me, the sunlight streaming through the window creates a mirage of his face. His voice, steady and unwavering, pushes away the shadows of doubt that linger in my mind. Each laugh we share feels like a gentle promise, a thread weaving our happy ever after closer with every passing moment.

I remember the way he holds my hand, fingers entwined, and acknowledge that we have faced the stormy seas of his challenges together. In those quiet moments, I feel an unshakeable sense of belief in him. The world can throw anything our way, but standing by his side, I feel an unyielding confidence resonate in my heart.

Memories of mornings filled with his laughter and evenings spent dreaming about our future paint a vivid picture of what we could be. I can see the sun setting behind us, casting a warm glow on the life we are building together. With every beat of my heart, I know we will find our way to that happy ever after, just as we have always imagined.

James and Alex have devised a scheme to use the funds initially raised for the tax bill to finance his escape, and the plans are in motion. James is confident that it will be less risky to leave Turkish territory via a road border. He is ready to journey by ferry to Turkish-occupied Northern Cyprus and then on to Southern Cyprus, from where he will fly to Zurich to sort out his finances so that he can repay everyone the money they have lent him.

The winter sun, still warm, bathes the square buildings of Ankara. James stands at the safe house door, his backpack slung over one shoulder. Alex takes a photograph, which James shares with me. He looks anxious, but the image accentuates his eyes, sparking like the fading daylight, igniting passion and excitement within me.

'Are you ready for this?' I ask, my heart racing.

'Ready as I'll ever be. Cyprus, here I come!' he responds.

A rush of warmth fills me, but my stomach tightens. 'You promise to call me the moment you arrive, right?'

'My darling, I'm coming home to spend the rest of my life with you,' he promises, his voice steady, though I catch a flicker of uncertainty beneath his bravado.

'Just remember, you're not in this alone – #bringhimhome, right?' I remind him, a wave of determination swelling between us.

'Always. You're my secret weapon, you know that?'

I swallow hard, trying to keep my emotions at bay. 'You make it sound easy. What if things don't go as planned?'

'They will. I believe it. And besides, you're with me in spirit. Nothing can break that.'

The familiar flutter of hope dances in my chest as I reach to touch his picture on my phone's screen. 'Promise me you'll stay safe.'

'Promise,' he says. 'I'm coming back to you. Just hold tight for me.'

A mix of excitement and nerves churns in my stomach as he attempts to end the call. 'Call me as soon as you are safe in Cyprus, okay?'

'I will. Just wait for that amazing ring that I will put on your finger when I get home,' he adds, the smoothness of his voice igniting something fierce inside me.

I stare at his picture again, and my heart swells with love and pride. 'Cyprus or bust!' I shout, unable to contain the thrill building inside me.

Even with the world's weight on him, my man stands tall, his smile a beacon of strength. 'You bet!' he replies, his voice steady and bright.

I can almost feel the energy of our shared dreams crackling in the air, guiding us on the adventure that awaits. And at this moment, I know that I have to be there to greet him on the other side, ready to turn our dreams into reality.

The phone disconnects, and I stand in my kitchen, dazed, the sounds of the world around me fading into the background.

'Are you okay?' My daughter Sarah glances over, her brows knitting together with genuine concern.

'I'm trying to be,' I say, my voice strained with the effort of maintaining composure. 'I just hope he's okay.'

She steps closer, her eyes searching mine. 'He said he would call you, right? So, he will.'

'Yeah, but...' I shift my weight, and the tension in my stomach tightens. 'What if he doesn't?'

'Then we face it together, one step at a time,' she replies, placing her hand gently on my arm. The warmth seeps through, comforting even in the chaos of my thoughts.

I glance at my phone on the table, its dark screen a stark reminder of the unknown. 'I just wish I could see into the future,' I mumble, my fear creeping into my voice.

'Sometimes the waiting is part of the journey.' She smiles gently. 'Think of it as... anticipation.'

'Torture might be a better word.' I chuckle softly, but the sound is heavier than I'd like.

'You love and trust him,' she reassures me. 'Give him the time he needs. Just breathe.'

I take a deep breath, letting her words settle over me. The fluttering in my stomach calms as hope sprouts amidst the fear. 'You're right. It's just... hard not to worry.'

There is so much that my beautiful daughter does not know about this situation, but with her beside me, I feel the weight of uncertainty lift just a little, and I let the flicker of hope grow slightly brighter.

James's Story, The Road to Cyprus:

It's New Year's Eve, and James's fingers drum an anxious rhythm against the steering wheel as the van's engine roars to life, cutting through the stillness of the early morning. 'You ready for this?' he asks, stealing glances at the rearview mirror, half expecting shadows to lurk behind them.

'Just keep your cool,' Samir, a trusty transporter that Alex has hired, says from the passenger seat, adjusting his UN cap with a confident flick. 'We've got this.'

James pulls onto the main road, taking a deep breath as adrenaline surges. The weight of uncertainty feels heavy as he recalls the stories of others who have taken this route – skirmishes, unforeseen checkpoints, and near misses. 'What if they know we're coming? What if there's a trap waiting for us?' he whispers, his heart pounding as darkened streets loom ahead.

Samir leans back and steadies his gaze. 'Tonight, they're too distracted with celebrations to worry about us. Just trust the plan.'

As they approach the first checkpoint, the menacing glow of flashing lights bounces off the night sky like a siren's call. James's grip on the wheel tightens, knuckles white with tension. 'Here goes nothing.'

'Remember the plan. Smile. We're just two medics returning from an assignment,' Samir urges, his calm demeanour grounding James amidst the chaos in his head.

James nods, forcing a grin as they roll up to the guard. 'Mutlu yillar!' he calls out, his words sharp and clear in well-practised Turkish, hoping to blend in with the local culture and ease any suspicion.

The guard squints at them momentarily, and the air is tense before he lazily waves them through. 'Mutlu yillar!' he replies, his indifference palpable. Realising that he has been holding his breath, James exhales, feeling the knot in his stomach loosen slightly.

'See? Easy,' Samir says, a hint of a smile playing on his lips as they navigate through the night. Each checkpoint passed boosts James's confidence.

Every flashing light they leave behind evokes a sense of freedom, however fleeting, that washes over them until they finally approach the port. The early morning light begins to paint the horizon, setting the scene for the final checkpoint at the ferry port, where they will embark and travel across to Cyprus.

'Last leg,' Samir states, determination returning to his voice. 'Let's make this count.'

James adjusts his cap, inhaling the crisp morning air. 'Time to look the part,' he says, swinging the van door open like a seasoned adventurer stepping into familiar territory.

A pulse of defiance surges as he steps out, dressed in his UN medic attire. 'Let's just hope they don't dig deeper than a glance or a simple New Year's greeting!' he jokes nervously.

'Just act naturally,' Samir reassures, eyes scanning the area for any signs of danger. 'We're professionals returning to base after a mission.'

James approaches the port official, a bravado he doesn't quite feel bubbling in his chest. 'Mutlu yillar!' he exclaims, enthusiasm masking his unease.

The official glances at the van, his scrutiny barely touching their uniforms. 'Go ahead,' he instructs, waving them through.

James can hardly believe it; fortune teases them with each passing moment.

As they board the ferry, the sun peaks across the horizon, and its golden rays dance on the water's surface. The thrill of adventure fills the air as James turns to Samir, a grin breaking across his face. 'That's the hard bit done, the border in Cyprus should be a breeze!'

'Oh yes, my friend! We have just taken a big step closer to your freedom,' Samir rejoices as they sail towards Northern Cyprus, hearts racing with the promise of new beginnings.

I stand in front of the departures board at Gatwick Airport, my heart racing with excitement and apprehension. The buzzing energy around me feels electric. 'This is it,' I whisper to myself, feeling a thrill – but also a weight of uncertainty. Surprising James in Cyprus seems like a beautiful idea, yet here I am, feeling the full force of my decision.

I glance at the other solo travellers as the plane ascends into the sky. Each face tells a story, but mine feels the most vulnerable. The anticipation of the surprise, the uncertainty of his reaction, and the fear of disappointment all swirl in my mind. I squint out the window, imagining the moment James sees me waiting for him, and the warmth of that thought brings both joy and anxiety. 'I can't wait to see you,' I murmur, biting my lip.

The warmth of the Cyprus winter sun caresses me as I step out of the cab at the hotel. 'Wow,' I breathe, overwhelmed by the vibrant coastal views. They are breathtaking, yet I feel a pang in my heart. My hotel room, though basic, holds its own charm. Flopping onto the worn wooden bed, I feel my early start catch up with me, and I close my eyes, wishing with all my heart that James was with me.

Hours later, sunlight streams through the flimsy curtains, gently waking me to a new day. 'James,' I whisper as I reach for my phone, my heart racing. 'Please pick up,' I plead quietly, but it goes straight to voicemail. I lay in my bed, expectant and excited, awaiting his return call. Two hours later, I am still waiting, and as time passes, my stomach twists – why hasn't he called? A wave of concern washes over me, and I resort to texting him, but the WhatsApp screen taunts me with a grey tick that refuses to double. James always calms my nerves in such situations with his infectious laughter and warm smile. However, his absence now only amplifies my worry.

The sun warms the crowded terraces of the resorts. I stroll past the vibrant turquoise pools, where laughter bubbles and glasses clink, an orchestra of joy playing around me. Each bar I pass boasts colourful lights, and fragments of lively conversations drift like whispers on the breeze. I catch a glimpse of my reflection in a polished window, where I stand as a shadow, just a spectator.

I need to eat, and the neatly laid table before me holds a plate of meze, untouched, the vivid colours of the dips and fresh bread stark against the empty chair across from me. The scents twirl around me – herbs, spices, and a hint of ocean salt – each inhalation a reminder of the feasts that could be shared, and the laughter that should be filling the air. I reach out to the plate, but my hands falter, and I retreat to a crinkled packet of crisps in my bag instead. The crunch echoes too loudly in the silence that surrounds me, each bite heavy with the weight of longing.

I scan the crowd, searching for a familiar face among the sea of strangers. My heart whispers a name that hangs in the air: James. Where are you?

I call his number repeatedly, nerves tightening with every unanswered call. 'Pick up, please,' I urge, frustration bubbling. But every time, it leads to voicemail. 'Damn it!' I exclaim softly, kicking at the floor in frustration. Desperation creeps in as I message friends from his circle. 'I just need to find him,' I type, hoping for a response, but silence answers. Each missed call and unanswered message gnaws at my heart, amplifying my anxiety.

My trip is only for four days, and the final day has arrived too soon. I have decided to spend this last day by taking a bus ride across the island. The landscape turns bleak as we near the Turkish border, and my heart sinks into the darkness of the huge potholes in the road. 'You got this,' I tell myself, seeking strength in my resolve. Yet, the stern faces of the guards, their cold and unyielding eyes, chip away at my courage.

'What is your business here?' one asks, his tone sharp. I take a breath, feeling incredibly small.

'Just... looking for someone important to me,' I manage. My voice quivers under the weight of emotion, and his indifference stings, leaving me feeling isolated and alone in this barren landscape. The walls seem to close in, and I accept that it was reckless of me to come here. I hastily retreat to my hotel, tears escaping as I gaze through the return bus's dust-covered window. 'Why, James?' I choke, my sobs carrying the weight of unfulfilled dreams and questions.

Packing to go home is overwhelmingly emotional. 'I just wanted to see him,' I whisper, stuffing clothes into the suitcase in a desperate rant. The burden of leaving without him weighs heavily on my soul. I glance at my phone one last time as I wait to board my flight home. 'Come on, just one message; please say something to stop me from getting on this plane and going home without you!' I silently plead. The single grey ticks against my countless messages stare back at me, cruelly unmoving.

'I guess I have to accept it,' I murmur, my voice thick with sadness, reality is settling around me like a heavy fog. Yet, deep down, hope still lingers.

Chapter Six – All That Glistens is Not Gold

James's Deception

The calm waters of the Turkish marina shimmer under the evening sun, casting a tranquil glow over the scene. James Anderson shuts down his burner phone and snips the SIM card in two, the screen darkening as he ends what he has decided is his last contact with Jane on New Year's Eve. As he removes any trace of their liaison with deft fingers, a flicker of warmth dances in his smile momentarily, but it swiftly vanishes, replaced by a cold, calculating smirk.

His laptop comes alive, revealing a spreadsheet filled with numbers and names. Each entry tracks the monies he's earned – five women across three counties in the UK. The figures rise as he glances through the rows, noting the steady cash flow each one provides. A sense of pride swells within him; he knows exactly when to pull back, when to stop. With a quick stroke, he tallies up Jane's transfers, and a wave of satisfaction washes over him, eclipsing any hint of guilt that dares to linger.

'Another thirty thousand,' he murmurs, reaching for his phone. It's time to recruit; Jane and a lady called Lucy are both now boring him, and don't appear to have any more cash, so it's time for them to go. Annabelle in Edinburgh is his latest recruit – she is proving good for a quick ten thousand when he applies the right pressure. She and Mary in London appear to be still willing to 'help', so they can come along as his journey of escape moves into the Mountains of Cyprus, where he will get shot and need emergency treatment which will need to be paid for. Then there is Jenny from Bristol; she is becoming a little tricky, so she will probably need to be replaced shortly. He will give her one more chance.

When he'd first met Jane, he'd flashed a charming smile, seamlessly transforming into James Warner, the attentive listener she'd craved. Each word he'd spoken had been carefully chosen, every gesture deliberate as he'd leaned in to catch her gaze, drawing her into his world.

With Lucy, the game shifted. He became James Wilson, a swift change in demeanour as he adjusted the cuff of his shirt, portraying a confidence that made her laugh. The way he tilted his head, feigning interest in her stories, revealed a practised ease. Her admiration was palpable, yet he knew he held the strings.

Annabelle found herself captivated by his charisma as James Young, his laughter infectious yet hollow. He could charm her with tales of daring adventures while balancing the accounts in his head, calculating profits that danced just out of sight.

For Mary, he transformed once again, taking on the persona of James Yates. Her worries faded as he wove a narrative of support and understanding, his attention a warm embrace that

LOVE, LIES AND BUTTERFLIES

tucked her insecurities away. Every compliment was a calculated investment in her affection.

Lastly, with Jenny, his façade shifted to James Thomas, the suave gentleman who made her feel seen and cherished. Each smile he flashed felt genuine, yet beneath it all, he was an actor in a play, the script penned with invisible ink only he could read.

James had a twin brother, Robert, who had died as a teenager.

Memories of their childhood haunted him – his brother's effortless charisma, the way girls would flock to him like bees to honey while James had stood by, a silent witness to a world that always seemed just out of his reach. This had allowed James's envy to twist and fester in his chest, sharp and bitter.

And so, when his marriage had broken up, a sinister game fuelled by anger and self-loathing had evolved. Each encounter felt like a carefully plotted move in a game where winning was everything. To the outside world, he was a master of seduction, but beneath the surface, a deeper plan unravelled. Every woman he carefully selected became another piece of his sprawling jigsaw, a stepping stone in a world he crafted meticulously. In seduction, there was power, a power he'd learned to wield like a maestro conducting an orchestra, turning charm and allure into a symphony that built his grand empire from the wreckage of his brother's fleeting memory.

Adjusting his aviator sunglasses, James smiles casually as he surveys the scene before him,

'Isn't she a beauty?' he says, nodding toward the sleek yacht rocking gently on the glassy blue water's surface.

The waiter, a young man with a friendly grin, follows his gaze. 'Is she your boat? 'Deception' is a great name.'

James nods, knowing well how the name resonates beyond mere words. The waiter adds, 'She is beautiful; you are a fortunate man.'

'Perfectly named,' James replies with a smooth chuckle. 'Just look at her – pristine white hull and that chrome shine.' He gestures exaggeratedly, tracing the yacht's elegant lines to ensnare the waiter's admiration. 'She's designed to catch eyes.'

'Are you planning to take her out today?' the waiter asks, pouring James a glass of chilled white wine. His eyes gleam with curiosity.

James takes a sip, hiding the sharpness of his ambition behind the wine's crisp, cool taste. 'Maybe. But why rush when the view here is so intoxicating? The water, the sunshine... these moments are for savouring.'

The waiter nods, perhaps sensing that the allure of the sea masks something deeper. 'True. But conquering the seas in that beauty sounds pretty special, too.'

James smirks, adjusting his expensive designer shirt as if it were armour. 'Oh, I do love a good thrill. But there's a fine line between thrill-seeking and being reckless, wouldn't you agree?'

At that moment, Clara appears – striking and magnetic, with sun-kissed hair and a smile hinting at a past full of life, love and heartbreak, and most definitely a potential gift to James's game.

'Enjoying the view?' she asks, leaning casually against the railing, her interest piqued.

James flashes his charm effortlessly. 'You could say that. I just acquired that beauty over there. I am James Devoir, by the way.'

'I'm Clara, and she's quite the catch,' Clara replies flirtatiously, her curiosity glimmering as she studies him with interest. 'What are you going to do with her?'

'Adventure, luxury, freedom.' He leans back, his tone smooth yet edged with an unspoken challenge. 'Sailing, living life on my terms. What could be more exhilarating?'

Clara's eyes sparkle with intrigue, but James also sees the flicker of caution. 'Sounds incredible. A fresh start?'

'Something like that,' he replies, his façade slipping ever so slightly as memories of Fiona, his ex-wife, the only woman he ever truly loved, and how she cruelly cast him aside, threaten to surface. These are moments he buries deep, afraid they will reveal his vulnerabilities and tarnish the allure he crafts for himself. 'But let's not dwell on the past. What about you? Which boat is yours, and do you have grand plans?'

Clara hesitates before admitting, 'Oh, I don't have a boat, can't even sail, but I'm just here on holiday, trying to rediscover myself after... well, you know how life can be.' Her eyes drift, revealing a vulnerability that James recognises as an opportunity. 'Divorce changes everything.'

'New chapters can be freeing,' he says, leaning in closer. Divorcees usually have a cash settlement in the bank, and his interest is now fully ignited. 'Have you ever thought about leaping into a new adventure?'

She raises an eyebrow, caution still etched on her face. 'Leaping has its risks. What about you?'

'I know how to play the game,' he replies, a hint of something darker lingering behind his smile. 'You learn quickly that it's all about doing what makes you feel alive!'

Clara chuckles, but he catches the flicker of vulnerability in her expression – a chance for him to weave his seductive web.

'I could show you the joys of spontaneity,' he suggests, his voice smooth as silk. 'How about dinner on Deception? A chance to escape the mundane?'

'Dinner on a yacht? That sounds alluring, but I hardly know you,' she muses cautiously. But as he flashes her a winning smile, her hesitance melts away. 'Alright, you've convinced me.'

As they talk, pleasure surges through him. This is familiar ground – he is weaving the illusion around her, the threads binding tighter with each moment. 'Perfect,' he says, savouring the sweet taste of manipulation taking root. 'I guarantee you won't regret it.'

Under the warm Turkish sun, the weight of memories tugs at him, but as he plans the next steps of his game with Clara, those memories fade like the dying light on the horizon. His posture remains rigid and calm – a mask for the heart that thuds inside him with unspoken words and untold lies. Shadows flicker in the corners of his mind, but the bright world around him blurs their outlines, allowing only the allure of Clara and the promise of his deceptions to shine through. He takes a deep breath, feeling the warmth envelop him, and enjoys a short reprieve from the tangled emotions that haunt him.

Peeling Back the Layers of Betrayal

'What has happened to James and why hasn't he called?' I whisper into the dimness of my bedroom, my voice trembling as I glance at the phone resting silently on the bedside table.

Each second that ticks by feels like an eternity, twisting my insides with worry.

'I don't know,' I murmur to myself, but the words are hollow, echoing in the space around me. 'What if something terrible has happened?' Panic tugs at my insides, a knot tightening in my stomach, clenching tighter as I tug at my hair, my fingers tangling in the messy strands.

The thunder outside rumbles ominously, a perfect reflection of the chaos in my mind. 'Maybe he's busy,' I say, my voice cracking under the weight of my desperation. The cold air stings my window, and the relentless rain keeps falling, drowning my heart.

I push back against the headboard, wishing for the soothing sound of James's voice, but I am only met with oppressive silence.

'Maybe he doesn't have a signal,' I mutter frantically, grasping at straws, 'and he'll just turn up at my door any minute now.' But even as I say it, the aching stillness from my phone feels like an anchor, dragging me deeper into despair.

It's been a month since my return from Cyprus – thirty long, agonising days where sleep evades me, and food holds no comfort. James's absence has turned my once vibrant life into a monotonous routine. My mood aligns perfectly with the oppressive, leaden winter skies outside, weighed down and heavy.

I still find myself repeatedly reaching for my phone, hoping against hope to see his name light up the screen. 'Come on, James,' I whisper, my voice barely audible in the silence that haunts me. The uncertainty tightens its grip on my heart, a vice-like pressure that refuses to let go. 'Please get in touch.

I can't bear the thought of never knowing what happened to you,' I plead.

Days and weeks stretch into an endless blur, and it's mid-morning one brighter day in late March when my phone buzzes sharply, slicing through the air and making me jump as adrenaline courses through me. I pounce on it, flashing my gaze at the unknown number. My heart races as I read the message:

'Do you know a man named James Wilson?'

I lift my phone for a better look at the screen, my fingers trembling as I scan the words. A surge of emotions crashes over me – hope, fear, dread. The realisation is jarring, and I can feel my heart thumping loudly against my ribcage as I read. 'It's been an eternity since I last heard from him – ever since he was supposed to return from Turkey.

– Lucy Webb'

I shake my head, disbelief sparking inside me. 'She sounds terrified. What if something happened to her James, or what if her James is the same as mine? This story feels too similar to be a coincidence.'

I pause, fingers hovering, wrestling with a whirlwind of thoughts. Taking a deep breath, I type: 'I know a James Warner who was supposed to return from Turkey in January but has just vanished without a trace. He hasn't been in touch, and this all sounds very similar. Do you think James Warner might be the same person as James Wilson?'

Silence stretches between us, and tension fills the space. Then Lucy sends an image that feels like a knife twisting in my gut. The man in her photo, showcasing that familiar smile, is unmistakably the man I have loved for the past three years.

James Wilson and James Warner are one and the same, and the realisation that I have been betrayed hits me like a freight train.

'Lucy,' I manage to type, my fingers trembling under the weight of the truth. 'I can't believe this. He's been lying to us both. We only live thirty miles apart, so we should meet, thrash this out face to face.' The sense of betrayal is overwhelming, threatening to drown me in its depths.

Her reply is slow, but when it does come, it is laced with the same heavy uncertainty I feel. 'I agree. We need to figure this out.' 'Thirty miles isn't far, right?' I mutter, the knot in my stomach tightening with each passing second. The thought of meeting Lucy sends chills down my spine. What if she's just another layer in James's intricate game of deception? The anxiety is palpable, a tempest raging within me.

I start pacing around my tiny house, the steady tick-tock of the clock reverberating louder with each passing second. I glance at my phone for what feels like the hundredth time, still hopelessly desperate for a message from James to tell me that it has all just been a big misunderstanding and quell the turmoil rising inside me. But the screen remains dark, devoid of any new messages.

Suddenly, my phone buzzes again, snapping me from my thoughts. My heart leaps, but it's not James; it's Lucy. 'I can't wait to see you tonight! We really need to get to the bottom of this.'

I type back with feigned enthusiasm, 'Yeah, me too!' while battling the despair and grief bubbling beneath the surface. I remind myself Lucy must be feeling just as lost.

'Oh, how could I have been such a fool?' I whisper, raking my fingers through my hair as the walls close in on me, amplifying my insecurities. The weight of my own naivety feels like a burden I can't shake off.

'Stop it,' I scold myself, shaking my head. The butterfly eggs that once held so much promise in my stomach morph into an anxious, vulnerable, ugly caterpillar. I can feel my heart pounding in my chest, my palms sweating. 'You're overthinking this,' I say.

As much as I tell myself to stay calm, the reality doesn't lie. The March chill sneaks under my turtleneck, sinking into my bones as I huddle over my laptop. The dim glow illuminates my worried expression, and I push away an empty coffee cup, squinting at the numbers on the screen.

'Oh my God, what have I done? I took out a loan and gave him all of my savings!' I mumble, desperation laced into my voice, wrapping around my throat like a noose.

Sarah, who is visiting me, pokes her head around the corner from the kitchen, concern etched on her face. 'What's the matter, Mum? You look like you've seen a ghost.'

I let out a hollow laugh, glancing back at her. 'Just the ghost of my empty savings account. It's haunting me.'

'Come on.' She steps into the room, arms crossed protectively. 'You need to breathe. It can't be that bad.'

'It's worse,' I say, feebly deleting the loan statement, desperate to conceal it from view as she moves closer for a hug. 'I'm drowning emotionally and financially.'

Sarah moves closer, her eyes scanning the now blank screen. 'Alright, let's not panic. I'm sure you'll figure something out, Mum. Look at how you rebuilt your life after Dad...'

'Thank you, darling,' I reply, my voice barely above a whisper, unable to break the silence surrounding us. I practice my smile, but the reflection in the glass windowpane reveals nothing but doubt. 'Just breathe,' I tell myself as the pit of humiliation threatens to swallow me whole. The day drags on, every passing moment tightening the vortex of despair, and all I can focus on is that thirty-mile drive ahead to meet Lucy.

As I stand teetering on the precipice of this revelation, I realise that this isn't just about a man who has failed us both. This is about a journey into the heart of deception, unravelling trust, and transforming our lives. Together, Lucy and I are about to cut through the darkness and unearth the truths that could redefine us – if we are brave enough to face them.

I park my car. Lucy stands before me, her vibrant, mismatched outfit popping against my plain jeans and polo-neck jumper. 'You really thought I'd wear something boring, didn't you?' She laughs, the sound echoing off the walls, contrasting with the chaos in my mind.

I shake my head, a reluctant smile breaking through. 'Honestly, I didn't know what to expect.'

With an arched eyebrow and eyes sparkling with mischief, she shoots back, 'Well, surprise! I'm probably not what you had in mind. Although you are exactly what I thought you'd be like!'

James's shadow looms, casting a pall over our tentative camaraderie as we order drinks, neither of us interested in food. I glance at Lucy, the anxiety bubbling up again. 'I still can't believe that he deceived me,' I mumble, feeling the heat rise to my cheeks.

'Oh, come on!' Lucy gently places her hand on my shoulder, her laughter ringing hollow yet comforting. 'He's in the wrong, and we will survive this!'

'I feel like such a fool,' I scoff, rolling my eyes, the truth biting harder than I expected.

'Yeah, two fools played by the same man!' she replies, shaking her head, yet a connection simmers beneath our shared embarrassment, creating a strange bond.

'I confronted him,' Lucy says, her words tumbling out in a rush. 'He answered the phone to you whilst I was with him and behaved really weirdly, trying to hide the call from me, but I saw your name – he said you were his mother's carer.'

Mystified and angry, we compare notes, and the puzzle pieces begin to fit with every revelation. It dawns on me that James never even boarded that plane to New York; he chose to go to Lucy instead.

Lucy's bravado falters as tears begin to spill over. 'He was so loving and had such a beautiful home. I thought everything was perfect. Now it's a complete disaster.'

We sit together for hours in the dimly lit corner of the pub, sharing pictures, memories, and the pain that binds us, our stories intertwining into an intricate tapestry of heartbreak.

'This isn't over,' Lucy asserts, a fierce determination igniting her eyes. 'We have to find him. I want my money back.'

I nod, a new fire igniting within me. 'We'll work with a private investigator. We can't let him get away with this.'

We are no longer just two women caught in the web of deceit, but a force united, ready to reclaim our lives and confront the man who stole from us. Together, we are stronger than the shame, and the truth will become our weapon as we set out to uncover who James really is.

As we prepare to leave the pub, I plaster a smile on my face, joining in the light-hearted banter, yet inside, a storm brews.

Every declaration of liberation feels like a jagged stone pressing into my chest.

As I drive home, the road blurs beneath my tyres, a dark ribbon winding into the night, but my thoughts race faster – memories of trust twisted into betrayal. The weight of it claws at my insides, rising like bile. By the time I pull over, the world outside spins erratically. I stumble out of my car, the cool night air biting into my skin, and lean against it; the metal is cold and unforgiving as nausea crashes over me like a wave, and I heave, the contents of my stomach spilling onto the verge. Each retch feels like another betrayal, another humiliation carved into me by the very man I once believed in. The taste of regret lingers in my vomit, sharp and bitter, as I pull myself together and continue on my journey home.

Chapter Seven – A Twisted Web

It's a week of reflection later, and sunlight glows over the chaos on my kitchen table. Papers and coffee cups huddle together, each bearing the weight of secrets and half-truths. Among them, a stack of documents, a laptop displaying incriminating emails, and a photo of a man who could be called James – who knows? Running a hand through my hair, my gaze bounces between the colourful collage of screenshots, photos, and Post-it notes scattered like confetti.

Lucy, now my friend and confidante, shakes her head, disbelief etched across her face. 'I can't believe we fell for this,' she says, her voice a mix of frustration and amusement.

I chuckle dryly, picking up a crumpled note. 'It's like we were blindfolded the whole time. Well, blinded by love anyway,' I reply, tossing the note back onto the table, the sense of betrayal heavy in my words.

'Seriously,' Lucy replies, her eyes wide. 'How did we not see it?'

'Look at this mess! All these signs were right in front of us. And yet...'

Lucy pauses, her brow furrowing as she studies the evidence. 'It's almost comical that we trusted him so much;

we should have known better. A terrifying thought has just struck me: do you think that we have unwittingly funded some criminal activity?'

I nod, tension and anger boiling. 'I hope not, but that's a scenario that we need to consider. We have also potentially helped a fugitive flee Turkey, if any of James's stories are true. We could get arrested, and we had better not plan to visit that part of the world until we know more about James and Alex and get some answers.'

'Oh, my goodness. I hadn't considered that.' Lucy shakes her head. 'Next time, I will be so much smarter – if I can even bring myself to face a next time.'

Lucy rifles through the documents and photos littering the table with purpose. 'We must be able to unravel this. My guess is that he is a creature of habit,' she declares.

A grin spreads across my lips. 'And he thought he could outsmart us?' I shake my head in disbelief. 'I can't wrap my head around that – there's no way we're letting him get away with it.'

'Seriously.' Lucy chuckles, rolling her eyes. 'Masterpiece was his online dating profile when I met him. What a ridiculous name! Does James, or whoever he is, really think he's some master of deception?'

'More like an evil con artist,' I reply, shaking my head. 'But now that we have all of this information, we can find a way to take back control. It feels incredibly cathartic doing this.' I flip through the pages of my pad, my expression intense. 'We were just pawns in his game, but these pawns are ready to bite back.'

Lucy shifts closer, her eyes sparkling with energy. 'We are just too emotionally involved in this and are going to constantly flip between victim and hunter; we need to get some expert help to track him down, to follow the money trail,' she says, her voice bubbling with anticipation. 'With the right help, we can find him – and his crew of crooks.'

'Absolutely! We can't let anyone else fall for his tricks,' I reply, slapping my palm against hers in a high-five. The sound echoes in the quiet room. 'We can do this.'

'Together,' Lucy nods, her jaw set with determination as she clenches her fist tightly. 'Let's bring him to justice.' She begins pacing as she mutters, 'We can't let him slip through our fingers. Not this time.'

I lean against the wall, crossing my arms and studying the pile of evidence on the table. Silence hangs heavy between us. The air in the room feels electric. I catch Lucy's eye as she bites her lip, twisting the hem of her shirt between her fingers. 'Lucy, what do you think James is doing right now?' I muse aloud. 'Those kids were laughing and playing in the sun on that video he sent you.' My voice is barely above a whisper as I watch them repeatedly in my mind's eye. 'Do you think that they are his?'

Lucy's eyes lock onto mine, her determination like a flame. 'I don't know, maybe it's all a façade. He could be living a double life. You know, the perfect husband at home, but a con artist elsewhere.'

I nod slowly. 'A family man, happy with a wife who has no clue...'

'Exactly!' she exclaims, anger bubbling beneath the surface. 'How could he do that to her – no... to us?'

A tingle creeps down my spine at the thought. 'An unsuspecting wife is a better outcome for us than an organised crime gang or antagonising the Turkish government, but I hate how I feel when I picture him with someone else. It's like this

LOVE, LIES AND BUTTERFLIES

jealousy is eating me alive, which is hard to reconcile, as I hate him and hope that he is dead.'

Lucy's expression shifts, resolve washing over her face. 'That's why we need to know the truth.' She halts mid-pace, turning to me, her eyes darting around, wide with unease. 'What if he's out there, watching us?'

I shudder at the thought, stealing a glance at the window. 'Just thinking about it... it makes my skin crawl. We should be the ones pulling the strings here. We have to find him.'

'If we let him get back into our heads, he wins,' Lucy shoots back, clenching her fists and drawing in a shaky breath. 'We owe it to ourselves to confront him. Whatever he's feeling, it sure isn't guilt. But we need closure.'

'Yeah, we do,' I reply, swallowing hard. 'We can't let this go on any longer.' The weight of the unknown will suffocate us.

Lucy goes home. We both need time together and time apart to process this, and tonight, my house bears silent witness to my unravelling as I sit on the floor, surrounded by every trace of James I can find – printed emails, photos, and gifts he'd given me. In the centre lay my bank statements, the evidence of my folly in cold numbers.

Thousands of pounds. Gone.

I reach for the wine bottle, but it is already empty, so I start on another. The room spins, and a very big part of me knows drinking alone on my bedroom floor at 3 AM isn't very smart, but I can't seem to stop.

I pick up my phone and scroll through our messages for the thousandth time. How can someone who didn't exist have felt so real? I trusted him completely. I loved him.

'You're pathetic,' I whisper, the words slurring. 'Fifty-five years old and you and your silly romantic notions have fallen for the oldest trick in the book.'

Lurching to my feet, I grab the nearest photo of us - one taken on the beach near here. With a cry that is half sob, half scream, I hurl it against the wall, the glass in the frame shattering spectacularly.

The violence of the sound shocks me back to myself. I stand there, barefoot amidst broken glass, wine-drunk and broken-hearted.

Rock bottom. This must be what it looks and feels like.

Eventually, I collapse into a drunken slumber. In the stillness, vivid images swirl in my mind – colours blend, shapes shift, and I drift deeper into my dream.

I'm in a room with James in my dream. I catch his glance, and his smile falters.

'What's on your mind?' he asks, concern etching his features. 'You look a little tense.'

James leans back in his chair, arms crossed, casual on the surface. 'It's natural to feel cautious when meeting someone new.'

'Exactly,' I murmur, my voice low. 'Can you ever really know another person, even if he seems perfect?'

His gaze sharpens, the playful facade slipping. 'I promise I'm just me. No tricks up my sleeve.'

I focus on him, really focus, and see his cold, calculating eyes trying to draw me in. A subtle smirk plays on his lips, camouflaging unspoken secrets. As I watch him, his disdain for women clings to him like a dark shadow, twisting his features into something monstrous.

'How do you find peace?' I ask. The thought of the stolen money gnaws at me – it isn't just the money; it's a theft of time, years ripped from the lives of others. I imagine the faces of those he's wronged, desperate and broken.

When you stand before a mirror, what do you see? A mask of confidence or the darkness lurking beneath? Do you confront that reflection, or are you too far gone to even notice?

Suddenly, I jolt awake, nausea curling in my stomach at the thought of him believing I'm pining for him. My fingers itch to get a message to him, to tell him that I most definitely am not!

I want to expose him and clarify that I see through his lies. I no longer view him as a soulmate but as the man who stands before me in my dream, a monster stripped of his disguise.

'It's time to make him pay!' I whisper to the shadows in my room. The weight of clarity settles across my chest, uninvited but necessary.

Tomorrow, Lucy and I will call an investigator. I don't think there is any chance I will get my money back, but I need to do something, anything, to feel less helpless and to start climbing out of this hole.

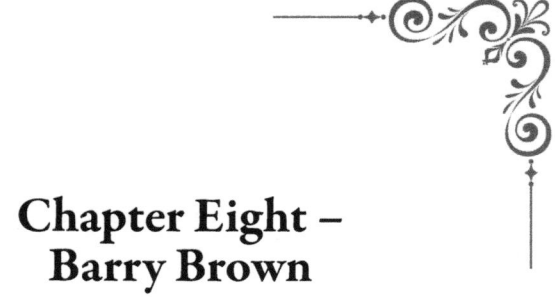

Chapter Eight – Barry Brown

Once again, Lucy and I sit in my kitchen, huddled around my open laptop. As the afternoon gives way to the evening, tabs of research on private investigators and scammers fill the screen.

'What about this guy?' Lucy leans closer, pointing at an investigator with very mixed reviews, her eyes wide with frustration. 'People are sharing their stories and –'

'Yeah, but some of those reviews are not good. What if he's just another scammer?' I shake my head, a knot twisting in my stomach. 'We've already been burned once.'

'True,' she replies, biting her lip. 'But we can't just sit here and do nothing. We need to appoint someone to help us find James.'

'Right,' I say, taking a deep breath. 'And we need our money back. It's not just about us – I would bet this house that he's scamming more victims as we speak.

'Look at this.' I gesture to a small article halfway down the Google search page. There are good reports about this guy...'

Barry Brown is a private investigator who specialises in tracking down fraudsters. My fingers race over the keyboard to share a page featuring a nice-looking man with kind eyes and, more importantly, a long list of glowing reviews. Perhaps he could be the one to help us.

'Yeah, listen to this: this Barry Brown recently took on a high-profile case for a TV show and solved it, bringing a romance fraudster based in Italy to justice. It could be a sign!' Lucy adds, and I catch the spark of hope shining in her eyes.

I swallow hard, apprehension creeping back in. 'But what if he doesn't believe us? What if he treats us like fools –'

'Hey,' Lucy cuts in sharply. 'If we don't ask, we'll never know. Let's schedule a consultation. The first one is free, and nothing ventured, nothing gained, right?' She smiles, her determination contagious. 'Let's give Barry Brown a call.'

As Lucy picks up her phone to make the call, I feel unease and excitement racing through me. Could this be our breakthrough?

Barry Brown is a vision in beige, with beige hair, beige skin, and a beige suit. However, I do notice his striking, large brown eyes and friendly smile as he stands near the large picture window in his immaculate office, bathed in the sunlight that bounces off the polished surfaces and sleek furnishings. Lucy and I sit stiffly on the plush suede-effect sofa, our eyes darting around the room, taking in the tastefully arranged artwork and elegant décor.

'Nice space, isn't it?' Barry is softly spoken, and his voice breaks the tension. 'I'm just a link in a very lucrative chain.'

Lucy raises an eyebrow, glancing at me. 'A private investigator working for a law firm? This isn't what we imagined.'

Barry pours three cups of steaming tea into matching corporate china mugs. The fragrant aroma swirls around us like a warm embrace as I take a sip, the hot liquid sliding down my throat, spreading a soothing warmth throughout my body and melting away my anxiety.

'I know it seems a bit opulent here, but I work with experts specialising in tackling fraud. We're dedicated to helping victims like you.'

'Victims,' I mutter, the weight of the word pressing down on me.

Barry's gaze is steady. 'I understand how tough this is. Many people feel ashamed after falling victim to romance fraud. I commend you both for coming forward.'

I look down at my hands, intertwining my fingers. 'Do you really think we can recover our money?'

'There's a good chance,' he replies softly, his voice steady, 'but remember, you're dealing with a professional fraudster. They're manipulative and clever.'

I shift on the sofa, my heart racing. 'So, what makes someone do this, Mr. Brown? How does it even begin?'

Barry glances at me, a thoughtful pause hanging in the air. 'Just call me Barry,' he says confidently. 'Usually, it's a mix of things. Sometimes, past hurts spark a craving for revenge. At other times, people are backed into a financial corner. And, sadly, some folks want to make a quick buck the easy way, at the expense of others.'

I press on. 'What about the man we both met initially? Do you think he's the same one we're dealing with online?'

Barry nods firmly. 'I think so, but I'll run his images through advanced facial recognition software and see if I can identify anything. It might help us understand who we're up against.'

I stare at the floor, momentarily lost in my memories. James seemed so... put together and happy. But was it hiding the darkness of a monster?

'Alright, let's dive into what we know about James W.,' I say, bouncing back to the present and glancing at Lucy, who also seems deep in thought.

'His family dynamics are a mess,' Lucy says, tapping her pencil against her notebook. 'Look at this – he told us about losing his parents and twin brother. That had to hit him hard. Plus, his marriage tanked because his wife, Fiona, I believe her name was, cheated on him with another woman, and she took their daughter to live with her.'

Barry scrolls through the timeline. 'That would shake someone who sees himself as a demigod. What about friends? Did he mention anyone close?'

I scan the screen, eyebrows knitted. 'Seems like he had barely any friends – mostly business associates. Maybe he was a loner? It could explain his behaviour now. But it also raises more questions. Why did he keep to himself? What was he hiding?'

Lucy's fingers trace the names of Alex Leo and a guy named Mehmet Genc – both connections James wanted us to send money to. 'We need to dig deeper into these guys. They could hold the key to finding him.'

'A timeline isn't just a list of dates,' I say, leaning forward, my fingers tracing the handwritten notes scattered across the table. 'It's a map of the facts we know about his life. We need to determine how these moments intersect.'

Barry's face is crumpled in concentration, scanning the details of James's profile that Lucy and I have created. And then a subtle smile breaks through. 'Wow,' he exclaims, his voice genuine. 'You two have really knocked this one out of the park. The level of detail here is impressive!'

Lucy bumps my arm with hers, her eyes sparkling with excitement. 'I told you we'd nail it,' she whispers, barely able to contain her glee.

Barry chuckles, warmth radiating from him. 'At this rate, I might have to offer you both jobs as my official researchers.'

Heat floods my cheeks, a flutter of flirty nerves mixing with the faint scent of his cologne wafting through the air. 'We're just glad to help,' I respond, trying to keep my tone casual but unable to hide the gratitude in my voice.

He laughs, the sound filling the space with a sense of camaraderie. As his strategic brain peels back the layers of James's life, each detail reveals more of the story, like a detective unravelling a mystery.

'Tell me more about the Cyprus story,' he says, his eyes locked onto mine, sending a jolt of energy through me.

I hesitate, glancing around the room. 'It's – well, it's complicated,' I reply, my voice faltering.

Barry leans in closer, his smile widening. 'Complicated? Those are the best kinds of stories. What happened with James?'

With a deep breath, I dive in. 'He told me that he was going to come out of hiding in Ankara and travel to Northern Cyprus with a transporter; they were going to get the ferry on New Year's Eve dressed as UN Medics, and that was the last that either of us heard from him.' The room is filled with a palpable tension as the story unfolds.

LOVE, LIES AND BUTTERFLIES 67

Barry nods, his curiosity piqued. 'He had really thought his story through, then?'

I can feel a knot tightening in my stomach. There's so much more than anyone knows, but I will not tell a soul about how I foolishly went to Cyprus to meet him. That is my secret, and I'll take it to my grave.

Barry's smile fades, replaced by a look of anticipation, drawing me deeper into the notes. 'So, who was James really, and did any of his stories actually happen? That is what we need to establish, and we need to do it now.'

I finally began to unravel the mystery tangled in my mind and accept that it's highly unlikely that any of it actually happened!

'You know,' Barry begins, stirring his drink absentmindedly, 'I've been thinking about James and the less adventurous stories that he shared.'

I raise an eyebrow. 'You mean the ones about his family? The lavish vacations, the fancy cars?'

'Exactly.' He sighs, running a hand through his hair. 'I can't shake the feeling that there's some truth buried in all that.' He pauses, glancing out the window as if searching for clarity in the bustle outside.

'Really? You think he's not just spinning tall tales?' I ask, my curiosity piqued.

Barry nods, his eyes narrowing in thought. 'Look, think about it. When fraudsters weave a lie, they often lace it with real details. It's like... It's like seasoning in a dish. It makes everything easier to swallow. Consistency is key, especially when you're juggling multiple victims.'

'Yeah, but isn't it risky?' I press, a sense of concern creeping into my voice.

'Yes, it is, but it works,' he replies, a hint of frustration in his voice. 'People are more likely to believe the unbelievable when they glimpse something familiar. It's not just a story; it's a carefully crafted web.' He looks me square in the eyes, determination flickering there. 'I'm reasonably sure there's a sliver of truth beneath all that chaos. He is a habitual liar and manipulator, which makes him dangerous.'

I contemplate his words, feeling their weight settle around us like the steam rising from our replenished cups of tea.

My eyes lock on Barry. There is an unexplained connection between us. I drum my fingers against the cool surface. 'I have a hunch,' I say, my focus unwavering as I glance at the images that James shared with us flickering on the screen before us. 'Our fraudster isn't from around here. He wouldn't risk being recognised by his victims when he is out with his family.'

Lucy raises an eyebrow, intrigued. 'So, you think he's from another part of the country?'

'Exactly,' I reply, my pulse quickening with excitement. 'If we dig into the backgrounds of those photos, we might uncover some clues. We need to find consistency in the locations.'

Lucy scribbles furiously in her notebook, her brow knitted in concentration. 'What about the money trail?' she asks, her gaze shifting to Barry.

Barry nods, his expression serious. 'Following the money is key. I'll ask the financial crime team to jump on this first. They have the techniques to trace stolen funds – bank statements, transaction records, etc.'

LOVE, LIES AND BUTTERFLIES

'Sounds promising,' I say, my eyes sparkling with determination. 'We need to catch this guy.'

'Absolutely,' Lucy and Barry echo, their voices in unison.

Barry leans in, his tone sharper. 'If we can identify the accounts he used to receive the money, we might pinpoint his location. There could be more evidence linking him to other crimes, too.'

Lucy crosses her arms, an unmistakable vulnerability in her stance, her eyes searching for assurance. 'Barry, do you think we've unwittingly become part of a crime by sending him money?'

Barry's expression hardens, conviction pouring from his words. 'I have a strong feeling that the story about the Turkish government is nothing but a fabrication. There's a lingering chance your money might have been funnelled into drugs at some point in the laundering process, but I hold onto the hope that it's merely been used to feed the insatiable greed of a sad, pathetic man. But mark my words, we must leave no stone unturned in this investigation. This fraudster believes he can play us for fools, but he's about to learn just how wrong he is.'

Lucy and I move through the multi-story car park after what has been an incredibly intense but strangely comforting meeting with Barry. The fluorescent lights flicker above us, and I catch the confusion and hurt swirling in her gaze. 'Are you okay?' I ask, gently tucking a stray hair behind her ear.

She nods, but I see the tremor in her lips. 'I need... I need some time to think,' she says, her voice barely above a whisper.

'Yeah, me too,' I reply, my heart heavy. 'It feels so raw, going over everything again. But I like Barry. I really believe we're doing the right thing.'

She raises an eyebrow, a teasing smirk breaking through the clouds. 'I noticed you liked him! You two sparked off each other. And no ring on his finger, either.'

I let out a soft laugh, rolling my eyes. 'Oh, come on! Just drive home safely, alright?' But I can't help the warmth that spreads in my chest.

'Always, and you, too!' Lucy winks, blowing me a kiss as she settles into the driver's seat of her Audi.

An investigator is appointed.

Barry returns to his desk, the light now casting long shadows across the scattered case notes. He flips through a stack of papers, brow furrowed, and mutters, 'There's got to be something in here.'

The murmur of colleagues' voices in the corridor fills the silence as he taps a pencil against his chin, eyes darting across the screen. 'Come on, think!' He pauses, flipping back to a particularly troubling part of the timeline, where a crucial piece of evidence seems to be missing.

'James W.,' he says aloud, the name heavy on his tongue. 'Do you think you can just walk away from this?'

The weight of Jane and Lucy's losses and the hurt they have been caused inspires him, and he arranges and rearranges the timeline taped to his whiteboard. 'You didn't just take their money,' he thinks, 'you took something far more precious: you took their trust.'

'I'll follow the trail, and I won't stop until justice is served!' he vows, eyes alight with purpose. 'I owe it to them and all of your other victims, past and present, of which I am certain there are many.'

Chapter Nine – Embracing the Chaos

Today, I have returned to Barry's office. We stand side by side, and the scent of board marker pens lingers in the air. His brow furrows as he studies the Post-it notes arrayed in a colourful and ever-expanding timeline winding its way like a snake across the whiteboard.

'Look at this,' he says, tapping the blue note at the top. 'This is where everything started for you.'

I lean in, tracing the edges of the notes with my finger. 'And this pink one – this is when he contacted Lucy?'

'Exactly!' Barry nods enthusiastically. 'But what about this yellow one, the Istanbul story? Shouldn't that be before the green one down here for Ankara?'

I tap the yellow note, glancing over at him. 'You're right. The Istanbul story, before Ankara. Let's move it up.'

Barry grabs a nearby marker. 'This is coming together much quicker than expected.'

'Yeah, it feels good to see it all laid out like this,' I reply, my eyes flitting across the timeline. The notes seem to pulse with energy, each a milestone in our journey.

Barry takes a step back, crossing his arms. 'We're making real progress. This guy is incredibly creative, and it's like we're mapping out a plot for a fiction novel.'

I smile, relishing the spark of collaboration. 'Let's keep building on this.'

The harsh chrome edging of Barry's large modern desk is pressing into my palms as I survey the unassigned Post-it notes spread out before me, each containing a comment or a memory, and a piece of the puzzle that demands to be placed. Lucy, who has by now joined us, huffs beside me, tapping her fingers impatiently. 'Can't you just let Barry do his job?'

I shake my head, thrilled at the progress that is gradually banishing the heavy past that's lingered for so long. 'I need to be part of this, Lucy. It's like a fog lifting inside my head.' Taking a deep breath, I feel the adrenaline spike. 'Do you really think we have enough to find him yet?' I ask the room, my voice steady, even as excitement flutters.

Lucy rolls her eyes dramatically, her smirk lightening her features. 'Give the man a break! We just appointed him. At this rate, he might pack his bags and tell us to take a hike!'

Barry chuckles, his eyes dancing as he meets my gaze. 'You might be onto something there! At this rate, I'll be applying for a leave of absence before lunch! Honestly, you've done an incredible job piecing everything together. Just keep the faith; we'll get him!'

A slow exhalation escapes me, and a warm and genuine smile breaks across my face. 'It's just... I can't remember the last time I felt like this. Like I can finally breathe.'

Barry's expression softens, a serious undertone to his words. 'This is the first step, Jane. You're not just surviving anymore; you're beginning to fight back.'

'I am,' I respond. 'There was a time I thought I would never escape this nightmare.'

Barry is a steady presence. 'It's been a long road but look at how far you both have come. You're smart, resilient, and focused on finding your way forward. Letting go of James will set you free,' he observes gently, his tone piercingly clear.

'We didn't just let go. We're ready to stop caring. James hurt us, but now we understand we deserve so much better.'

Barry raises his eyebrows, pride evident in his gaze. 'That's the spirit! You can't let him hold you back any longer.'

'No more humiliation,' I assert, my voice steady and strong. 'I'm ready to move on. No more looking back.' Lucy nods in agreement, her support reinforcing my resolve.

A proud smile spreads across Barry's face. 'That sounds brilliant; let's tackle whatever comes next together.'

'Together,' we affirm. The word is a team hug, a lifeline. As strength surges through me, I repeat, 'I'm ready.'

Later in the day, as I settle into my favourite spot on the beach, the sun kisses and caresses my skin, and the gentle waves tease the shore a few feet away. I bury my toes deep into the sand, relishing the coolness. The rhythmic crashing of the waves soothes my restless thoughts, but despite my earlier affirmations, the shadow of James lingers, nagging at the darkest corners of my heart.

A familiar voice cuts through the air, drawing my attention. "Hey! I had a feeling I'd find you here! Mind if I tag along?" It's Barry, his tone light and teasing as he makes his way over. Dressed in shorts and a T-shirt, he looks refreshingly different, far from his usual plain self. With each step he takes, clouds of soft sand swirl around his feet, giving him an almost comical, carefree look.

I look up, a coy smile spreading across my face. 'Only if you promise to make this moment even better,' I tease.

Barry plops down beside me, stealing a glance at the sea. 'What's on your mind? You look like you're dreaming about something, or someone.'

I shrug, my gaze drifting to the horizon. 'Just... pondering life, and, you know, the mistakes we make.'

He chuckles, leaning a bit closer. 'We all make them. It's how we learn. But trust me, you're not going to meet another James. You're way too smart for that.'

I can't help but grin, feigning a dramatic sigh. 'What if I end up making the same mistakes? How do I know I won't fall for someone equally charming and manipulative?'

'Trust is tricky,' Barry replies, his eyes sparkling with mischief. 'But don't let the ghost of James keep you shackled. You're stunning, smart and have so much to give a relationship and deserve to find a man who truly appreciates you for who you really are.'

I bite my lip, a flutter of excitement and nerves dancing in my stomach. 'You really think I'm all those things?' I ask, my voice teasingly flirtatious.

'Absolutely,' Barry says, his gaze locking onto mine, intensity flashing in his chestnut brown eyes. 'You're stronger and more captivating than your doubts. Plus, life's too short to be scared of happiness.'

LOVE, LIES AND BUTTERFLIES 75

His words linger in the air playfully as he leans in, wrapping his arm around me in a warm, comforting embrace. I can feel my heart race, the memories of James beginning to fade away in the sanctuary of his presence. 'Maybe you're right,' I say softly, glancing up at him with a hint of mischief in my eyes. 'I just need to find the right man to help me take that leap.'

As Barry's arm settles around my shoulders, a familiar warmth spreads through me, softening the corners of my thoughts. Yet, mingling with that warmth is an unsettling realisation: this feeling isn't new. It mirrors the comfort, the immediate trust I once felt with James – different man, identical sensation.

It stirs questions within me about the nature of connection and how easily one can slip back into old comforts, even when the faces change. What does this mean for me? For the choices I have yet to make? I can't help but wonder if I'm merely chasing familiarity, or if there's something deeper waiting to be discovered.

'Everything okay?' Barry asks, his concern evident as he picks up on my sudden tension.

I instinctively nod, but inside, a warning bell tolls loudly. How can I rely on this feeling when it has led me astray before? Am I just shifting my need for security from one person to another without truly healing?

'Just thinking,' I finally reply. 'About how quickly I tend to trust. It's something I really need to be mindful of.'

Barry nods, his arm still around me, and I don't ask him to remove it – at least not yet. I make a mental note to take my time this time around, to stay alert to the signs I've overlooked in the past. The warmth of his embrace is comforting, but I know that comfort doesn't always equate to safety.

'That's because you are a wonderful, kind, caring woman. Embrace who you are, and don't let him take that from you!' Barry adds as he playfully pulls me deeper into his hug, and I can't help but giggle, needing to ease the tension.

'Embrace the chaos, huh? Sounds a bit reckless.'

'It can be.' He chuckles, letting go just enough to look into my eyes. 'But sometimes, that's where the magic happens.'

I return to basking in the sun's warmth as our spark ignites.

Lucy and I meet weekly, and today, as the warm afternoon sun spills through the cafe's shutters, painting patterns on the floor, I notice that my friend seems stressed. 'Are you okay?' I ask as I watch her shuffle papers on the table.

Lucy glances up, a forced smile barely masking her worry. 'Yeah, just... You know, the usual. Bills and loans,' she mutters, her fingers tapping nervously on the papers in front of her.

I am compelled to place a comforting hand on Lucy's arm. 'You don't always have to handle this alone, you know? I'm here for you.'

Lucy sighs, leaning back in her chair. 'It feels like a never-ending cycle. I'm so angry with myself for taking out that loan for James, and now I'm stuck in a financial hole. What if Barry can't get the money back?' Her voice quivers.

'I know it's tough; it's the same for me,' I reply softly, squeezing my friend's hand. 'But remember how far we've come. We'll figure it out together. You're not alone in this.'

'Thanks, Jane,' Lucy says, a hint of gratitude breaking through her distress. I don't want to drag you down with me; you seem much stronger than I am.'

'You could never drag me down,' I insist, eyes shining sincerely. 'Together, with Barry's help, we'll face whatever comes next. What's one more challenge for us?'

Lucy chuckles lightly, the tension in her shoulders beginning to ease. 'Yeah, I guess that's true. I need to focus on the brighter side, right?'

'Absolutely. Let's take it one step at a time,' I reply. 'Now, how about a cup of tea and some chocolate? We need to treat ourselves, and it's my treat!'

With that, Lucy nods, her expression softening as a glimmer of hope flickers in her eyes. 'Okay, that sounds perfect.'

Lucy leans closer, a teasing smile playing on her lips, her eyes sparkling with mischief. 'So, are you and Barry an item yet?'

I shake my head, a teasing blush creeping up my cheeks. 'Not yet,' I say, my voice playful, like I'm sharing a delicious secret. 'But... I feel a spark with him. Hanging out together is always a blast.' A coy smile curves my lips as I add, 'We're sliding into very good friends territory – who knows where it might go?'

Lucy raises an eyebrow, the playful glimmer in her gaze deepening. 'I knew it! You two have that whole flirty vibe going on, he's a great guy – your heart would be in safe hands with him,' she says, her tone layered with a hint of envy, but mostly warmth. 'If anyone deserves a nice guy, it's you, Jane.'

'We both do!' I exclaim.

Suddenly, a tall figure strides into the café, and dread tightens in my chest as I notice how his side profile echoes James's. I catch Lucy's eye, her gaze instinctively flicking toward the counter where the man stands. His back turned to us, he is shrouded in a chilly air of familiarity.

'He looks just like him,' I whisper, leaning in, my voice barely above a tremor.

Lucy shakes her head, but her body tenses, betraying her resolve. 'It's probably nothing. Just someone unfortunate enough to look like a fraudster,' she tries to reassure us both, but her words feel thin against the heavy atmosphere.

'Nothing?' I scoff, desperation creeping into my tone. 'We have to be careful. Barry warned us – if James finds out we're looking for him...' My words hang in the air, oppressive and threatening, like a dark shadow looming over us.

'He won't intimidate us,' Lucy interjects, the steel creeping into her voice doing little to mask her apprehension. 'We're in control here,' she insists, though I can hear the uncertainty beneath her bravado.

The man at the counter pivots, and a wave of relief floods through me as his face comes into view. I am braced to confront James, but thankfully, this stranger is unknown to me. Yet as I glance at Lucy, her eyes are wide, mirroring my own fear as we cradle our cups, the warm liquid doing little to thaw the chill that grips us.

This moment is a brutal reminder that we never truly know who lurks in the shadows. Danger may be just around the corner, unseen yet ever-present, and our hearts pound in a frantic rhythm – an anxious symphony of anxiety binding us in a tight grip of uneasy safety.

Chapter Ten – The Investigation

A month has passed since we appointed Barry, and today is our first full team update. I am not going to lie. I've made a bit more of an effort with my outfit and makeup than usual. Barry Brown is still just a friend, but he becomes more attractive to me every time I see him, and this morning, he looks great in an M&S rather than a Ralph Lauren kind of way. As he leans forward, his eyes sparkle with enthusiasm as he announces, 'Alright, team, let's dive in.' He flips open his laptop and skilfully projects the report onto the large screen on the wall.

I shift in my seat, curiosity piqued. 'I can't wait to hear what you found in Turkey!'

Barry's smile widens. 'You won't believe this! We have checked all five addresses you provided. Turns out, they're all shops or offices.' He points to the map on the screen. 'Four of them are completely vacant, but the fifth. It's a doctor's surgery!'

Lucy is immediately intrigued. 'Interesting. Did you learn anything about the tenants?'

'Absolutely,' Barry replies, his excitement building. 'We discovered a guy named Mehmet Genc used to rent the surgery.' He glances at Jane, raising an eyebrow. 'James claimed Genc was one of his associates.'

I involuntarily cross my arms as my interest intensifies. 'Do we have more on him?'

Barry nods, tapping the keyboard. 'The current tenants gave us Genc's home and business addresses. We're one step closer to discovering the truth!'

Lucy leans in, her voice barely above a whisper. 'This could lead us to James.'

Barry spins a grin across his face. 'It most definitely could!' He straightens up, the energy in the room shifting. 'Mr. Genc is already under investigation for corporate fraud. The Turkish police are eager to review our evidence regarding this additional violation.'

I am hanging on his every word. 'What else do we know?'

Barry's expression becomes serious as he continues, 'He has been interrogated and is now scrambling for excuses. Can you believe it? He claims he was 'doing a favour for a friend' by handling money from clients, who, coincidentally, were all women.'

'What?' I gasp, eyes wide. 'How many women?'

'Several,' Barry replies, nodding. 'He says a man named Alex Leo set everything up for him. This Alex character is reportedly working under the guise of helping businesswomen relocate to Turkey.'

'Alex Leo, the solicitor?' I exclaim, a mixture of shock and intrigue washing over me.

'Exactly,' Barry affirms, his voice steady. 'Genc receives payments into his US dollar business accounts, then hands out the cash to Alex Leo after taking his cut. After that, he claims he does not know where the money goes.'

Lucy fidgets, her mind racing. 'What happens next?'

Barry leans back in his chair, a hint of satisfaction creeping into his tone. 'The Turkish authorities are now involved. They've already tracked down Alex Leo and have brought him in for questioning.'

Silence envelops us as we contemplate the unfolding web of deceit.

Barry's eyes meet mine as I sit, shocked, digesting the revelation that Alex Leo is not a solicitor, but more of an underworld fixer!

Alex Leo

The air in the Istanbul hotel bar buzzes with a symphony of clinking glasses and low conversations. Alex Leo leans back, a devil-may-care smirk dancing on his lips. He swirls the whiskey in his glass as his eyes dart across the room like a hawk searching for prey.

James, the Englishman sitting across the table, leans in closer, eyebrows raised. 'So, you're telling me that business has been tough? Is that why you're stuck in this... charming little joint?'

'Charming? You must be joking.' Alex chuckles, lowering his voice as if sharing a secret. 'The truth is, it's been a nightmare, mate. The pandemic hit hard – lost clients, dwindling funds.' He pauses, his gaze sharp. 'But I've got a plan.'

James's interest is piqued. 'A plan? This I have got to hear.'

'It's all about discretion,' Alex continues, his tone smooth like the whiskey. 'Cash transactions, no questions asked. I see myself as

a fixer for clients who want to receive money without attracting unwanted attention.'

James considers. 'Let me get this straight: you think you can offer a middle-man cash handler service that will protect my identity?'

'Protection, yes. For a small fee, I can guarantee you complete anonymity,' Alex says, a playful glint in his eyes. 'I've navigated this chaos better than most. Thought I'd be drowning but look at me – still swimming.'

James's lips curl into a smirk. 'You've got a gift for spotting an opportunity, I'll give you that, Alex.'

'I know your line of business. I am currently setting up a process to assist six others whose income is generated in the same way as yours. I've got contacts, and, as you say, a knack for recognising opportunity, my friend,' Alex replies, lifting his glass and making a mock toast. 'Partnerships!'

And so, a twisted arrangement is cemented over the clinking of two glasses filled with whiskey over ice.

Alex orchestrates a scheme that blends legitimate banking with shady dealings. With each deal, a portion of the funds flows into his pockets, masked by a veneer of respectability. He revels in the thrill of it all, seeing each transaction as another step toward building a fortune that glitters far beyond his current means.

Alex's insatiable greed fuels his insatiable mind, which races with plans. He has filled his spaces with lavish furniture and the latest gadgets, most fake designer brands, but each item a testament to his ambition. Yet shadows lurk in the corners of his success, whispers of illegality and tax evasion brushing against his consciousness like an unwelcome breeze. He brushes them aside, not wanting to tarnish the gilded image he is carefully crafting.

Then comes the day when the police descend upon him, their presence like a cold winter draught sweeping through his carefully constructed facade. Confident denial slips from Alex's lips as he contradicts the officers, insisting he is merely a victim of circumstance. Yet, the inevitable unravelling begins as they examine his computer and phone. The messages and connections lay bare his operations, revealing the extent of his betrayal, not just to the system but to those who had trusted him.

As the interrogation proceeds, Alex's bravado begins to wane. Faced with undeniable evidence and an insurmountable weight of guilt, he backtracks. Desperation morphs into self-preservation; he throws James and the other fraudsters on his client list under the bus, painting a picture of partnerships driven by coercion rather than his ambition.

Barry's tone shifts to serious. 'We haven't found James yet.'

My excitement fades slightly as I fidget with my notebook. 'I know... But what about the UK leads?' I ask, still shaken by the recent episode in the cafe.

Barry shrugs, a hint of frustration in his voice. 'Not much yet, I'm afraid. He covers his tracks well, but we won't give up! Oh, and guess what?' Barry's expression brightens again. 'During the dating site investigation, a lady has come forward. She said she's currently dating a guy who is using the same profile pictures.'

'What?!' I gasp, shocked. 'Do you think she could be another victim?'

'I suspect so,' Barry replies, his brow furrowed. 'I've set up a meeting with her to gather more information. I'll keep you updated.'

As the meeting wraps up, I feel frozen to my core. 'I can't believe it,' I mutter. 'James isn't just dabbling in romance fraud – he's deceiving women on an industrial scale. And it sounds like we have uncovered a whole network of romance fraudsters.'

'Exactly,' Lucy agrees, her voice low. 'This is so much more serious than we thought.'

Maggie

Maggie stands at the window of her bright Georgian terraced house, her heart racing as she glances at the clock. With a sharp breath, she opens the door when she hears a soft knock, and Barry is met with wide-eyed eagerness and a hint of defiance as she ushers him inside swiftly, casting a worried glance over her shoulder to ensure no prying neighbours see him enter.

As Barry sinks deep into her chintzy armchair, Maggie squares her shoulders and perches defiantly on the edge of an upright seat. Her posture is unwavering, though her fingers tap anxiously against the hem of her blouse. With steely determination, she launches into her rehearsed speech, the words bursting forth like a challenge: 'I know James is not a fraud. He's the most wonderful man I've ever met, and I won't let anyone say otherwise.'

Barry nods, keeping his expression neutral. He sees her firm conviction, the warmth spilling from her words as she recounts their idealistic month together – the laughter shared, the places they visit. With each memory, the tension in her shoulders seems to dissipate, only to return as she passionately defends James's character. 'He's a gentleman. He loves me.' Her eyes sparkle with resolve; her chin raises as if daring anyone to challenge her belief.

Yet, a subtle shift occurs when she reveals that James is stranded in Turkey, needing money to pay a tax bill. The light in her green eyes flickers as Barry feels the weight of the situation bear down on them like a thick fog. He listens as she brushes aside standard warnings about sending money to people she meets online, her voice firm in denial. 'He's real, we have met, and we're going to be together again!'

As she speaks, Barry fights to maintain his composure, knowing the truth awaits them both, lurking just beneath the surface of her fervour. Sensing the tension in the air, he decides it's time to share the stories of Jane and Lucy – two women who once shared the same beliefs.

Maggie's vulnerability settles on him as he gently opens his laptop and shows her the texts and photographs – evidence of Jane and Lucy's heartbreak and deception. The transformation is immediate. Maggie's face contorts; her confident façade crumbles as the reality of betrayal washes over her like a veil of sudden chill. Tears begin to stream down her cheeks, and her breath hitches as if the air has been stolen from her lungs.

'How could I have been so foolish?' she whispers, her voice trembling. Her own phone slips from her grasp as she offers it to Barry, yet another screen filled with desperate messages laced with heart emojis and pleas for help. He scans the messages carefully, noting the shift in tone from flirtation to demanding urgency, a darker side of James's manipulation unfurling before them.

Barry proposes a meeting with Lucy and Jane, a chance for Maggie to connect with those who have faced similar pains. But her eyes dim, and she shakes her head, needing space to process the storm roiling within her. 'I can't. I just... I need to think.' Her voice has a rawness and a tug of vulnerability that resonates deeply.

Yet, in that moment of despair, she extends her trust. 'I want you to recover my money. I will help in any way I can.' Determination flickers in her eyes, igniting a fire that refuses to be extinguished. Barry acknowledges her bravery, recognising the potential for her involvement to draw James out into the open.

Before leaving, he requests that she keep communicating with the fraudster and play along without sending more money. As Barry returns to his office, he can't shake the haunting image of Maggie's face, a blend of hope and despair forever altered by a fleeting love that masks the cruel reality of deception.

Chapter Eleven – The Sting

The concrete walls of the interview room reverberate with the low murmur of conversation, and investigators' eyes are firmly locked on Alex Leo, who shifts in his chair, a bead of sweat trickling down his temple.

Stung

'Look, Alex,' one investigator says, his voice steady but firm. 'If you cooperate with us, we can make this easier for you,' he continues, hinting at a reduced sentence in exchange for cooperation.

Alex swallows hard, glancing at the plain table between them. 'What do you want to know?' His voice trembles slightly, betraying his nerves.

'Just the truth about the nest of vipers that you have been facilitating with your schemes,' the other investigator replies, leaning intimidatingly close. 'Tell us about the money laundering scheme you devised, and the lowlifes who have used it.'

Alex bites his lip, the weight of their offer bearing down on him. 'And if I do?' he asks, his eyes darting between them.

'We can help you; put in a good word for you,' the first investigator assures him. 'But you need to give us something to work with.'

A frown creases Alex's brow as thoughts race through his mind like a runaway train. He reflects on the steady cash flow from the fraudulent enterprise, its allure drawing him in. But the chill of reality settles in, heavy as a winter's night.

'Why am I even considering this?' he mutters, running a hand through neatly cut jet black hair. Alex is vain, and his appearance is especially important to him; the very real reality of being forced to exchange his well-manicured appearance for one of greyness in prison attire is not lost on him.

Drawing a deep breath, Alex straightens, attempting to shake the weight from his shoulders. 'I will help you.' The steadiness in his voice feels more like an act of duty than genuine conviction. The investigators nod with evident pleasure. And Alex begins to pace the room, aware that he's taking on a role he never wanted. 'Here's what I remember,' he says, trying to inject some enthusiasm into his tone, but the effort feels hollow. 'They're not as smart as they think.' Each detail flows from him, pieces of information he's reluctantly remembered, like breadcrumbs leading deeper into a trap in which he is ensnared. He feels the spotlight on him; it's suffocating. Alex Leo longs to fade back into the shadows.

In the quiet corners of his mind, a stark realisation sets in. The promised cash flow, once a source of hope, now feels like a mirage that will evaporate before he can grasp it. The supposed allies now loom like spectres of betrayal. The shift from partners to adversaries is unsettling, and as he grapples with the plot twist, resignation washes over him, and he wonders if there's any way to rewrite this tale and salvage his reputation and livelihood.

'I was just a pawn in this game,' he says, bitterness and fear creeping into his tone. *'They will turn on me. You have to protect me and my family.'* Alex's tone of voice grows vulnerable, fuelled by fear. *'I'm afraid of what they will do if they find out that I have spoken to you,'* he declares; the arrest has rattled him badly. *'I will need your help to reclaim my future.'*

As he talks, his phone vibrates softly against the desk, the gentle hum slicing through the tense air of the interview room. He glances down, and his heart quickens as James's name glows on the screen.

'Should I pick it up?' he mutters to himself, fingers hovering uncertainly over the screen.

'If I don't answer, it'll raise suspicion. But if I do...' His voice trails off awkwardly, leaving an uncomfortable silence lingering in the air.

The phone vibrates again insistently. *'What if this is another transaction request?'* he mumbles, his mind racing.

The investigator, peering curiously at him, nods. *'Uh, yeah, go ahead and answer it. Just, you know, keep it cool. We can't let him know we're onto him,'* he says.

With a shaky breath, Alex straightens his posture, but he can't shake the feeling of all eyes on him. *'Okay, here we go,'* he mutters, sounding less confident than he wishes.

He finally taps the answer button, then fumbles the phone slightly, nearly dropping it. *'Hey, uh, James,'* he stammers, voice a bit higher than usual, betraying a slight tremor in his hand. *'How are things... um, on your end? Do you... uh, need the bank details to accept funds or something?'*

He winces at his awkwardness, feeling the weight of the investigator's gaze, and silently curses himself for sounding so nervous.

Alex clenches the edge of the table, his knuckles turning white. He can almost feel his racing heartbeat pulsing through the phone. After what feels like an eternity, James's voice slices through, cool and clipped.

'Yeah, please, I need an account to receive £25,000 worth of US dollars, which I then need you to send to me in Spain in Euros in three equal payments over a week. It's coming from the UK; get it done as soon as you can.'

'I'm on it and will get right back to you!' Alex replies with a tightened jaw; he hates James's condescending tone and how he speaks, as if handing down decrees, each word laced with sharpness and disrespect. Does James not realise the depths of the trouble Alex is wading through to accommodate him? Gratitude is absent, replaced by an air of entitlement, which leaves Alex simmering in silence as he settles back into his chair, ending the call and glancing at the officer beside him.

Less than an hour later, sweat beads gather on his forehead as he is typing the bank details the investigator has handed him into an email for James.

'Remember, Alex, we cannot afford to lose control of this money.'

'Make sure it's in the same format as usual,' *the officer presses, shifting his weight beside him.*

'Trust me. I've done this before,' *Alex snaps back.*

The officer narrows his eyes, but Alex can see a hint of understanding. 'Just... keep it transparent. This is crucial.'

Alex nods, pushing through the waves of doubt. He breathes slowly, watching the progress bar as the email is sent to James. 'There we go,' he mutters.

Three days later, Alex and the investigators are sitting in the same room, and the atmosphere is electric with anticipation. All eyes are locked on the screen, waiting for confirmation from the bank that the funds have arrived in the police suspense account.

'It's here!' one of his officers exclaims, barely containing his excitement.

'Steady,' Alex says.

The officer stands close by, eyes narrowing as the digital funds solidify in the designated recipient account.

'Yeah, I see it. Good work, all!' the officer finally says, allowing a cautious smile to remind the room that they must keep sight of this and maintain a line of control at all times.

Having received Alex's confirmation that the first instalment of the funds is now available for him to collect, James steps into the familiar Western Union branch, the bell above the door chiming cheerfully. The rich aroma of freshly brewed coffee fills the air, blending with the soft buzz of conversations and the gentle rustle of papers as the shop doubles as a café.

'Good morning!' the clerk says, her bright smile lighting up her face. 'How can I help you today?' Her eyes shimmer with curiosity as she leans forward.

'Just collecting some cash,' James responds, grinning wider as he pulls out a crumpled payment reference and slides the paper towards her.

The clerk's fingers fly over the keyboard as she processes the transaction. 'Got it. Just a moment, please,' she says, her voice light.

James shifts his weight, leaning against the counter, the rhythmic tapping of his fingers echoing in his mind. But just then, a notification buzzes on a nearby screen, slicing through the calm. He catches the cashier's tense tone as she whispers urgently to her colleague. His heart quickens, anxiety creeping in.

'Is everything okay?' he asks, glancing through the screen at their intense exchange.

'Uh, yeah, just a little something that needs checking,' the cashier replies, forcing a smile that doesn't quite reach her eyes.

A knot tightens in his stomach. With an instinctual urge to escape, he steps back, retreating into the shadows of the shop. He pushes the door open, the sunlight washing over him as he slides outside. Seeking refuge, he hurries to the nearby palm tree, its leafy canopy offering him a brief respite as he tries to steady his racing heart.

From his concealed vantage point, James witnesses chaos unfold as local police flood the shop entrance through which he has just escaped. Their uniforms blur into a frantic sea of blue, urgency radiating in their grim faces. Each determined step and tense expression intensify the atmosphere as if time has slowed.

'Shit, shit, shit! They're trying to trap me!' he exclaims, disbelief lacing his voice. He pushes away from the comforting shade of the tree, heart racing as adrenaline surges through him, and his long legs propel him along the narrow alleyways that stretch before him like a maze. He sprints between the buildings, each footfall echoing his panic. The shouts of the police officers fade into the background as he races toward his sanctuary – his boat, Deception.

'Come on, come on,' he mutters, urgency driving him forward – the familiar sight of his boat gleams in the sunshine, a beacon of safety before him.

Once onboard, he paces the luxurious cabin of Deception with his hands clenched into fists. Each step thumps against the polished wooden floor, perfectly matching the quickening beat of his heart. 'This isn't happening,' he mutters through gritted teeth, the words barely masking the fury bubbling beneath his skin.

He slams his palm on the table, and multiple phone handsets scatter like leaves in an autumn gust. 'Damn it!' he barks, his voice reverberating through the boat. Thoughts of betrayal flash through his mind, igniting a fire in his chest that he can't extinguish.

'Hey! Keep it down!' A voice in his head. The shadowy figure of his dead twin, Robert, is talking to him from the grave.

He stops, glancing at the mess of phones scattered across the floor. 'I can't think,' he replies, breathless, frustration cracking his voice.

A chill sweeps through him. James glances around, suddenly feeling claustrophobic in the luxury of the cabin. 'What's done is done,' he whispers, his heart sinking. The remnants of his reckless decisions loom large in his mind – he's left a trail, and the weight of being a wanted man settles heavily upon his shoulders.

'You were foolish and now have to figure out your next move carefully,' his imagined brother's voice instructs. James nods slowly, the reality crashing over him like a cold shower. 'Yeah, I do,' he replies to the emptiness.

Chapter Twelve – And Suddenly ...

James Re-emerges

The investigation has been maddeningly silent for weeks, a tense lull that hinted at something brewing beneath the surface. It has now become apparent that James has somehow escaped Spain, and the moment we've been waiting for has finally arrived—he has re-emerged, seeking answers with boiling fury. His message to Alex is laced with accusations and threats, demanding to know where everything has gone wrong.

Under the watchful eyes of the investigators, Alex is instructed to weave an elaborate story about a criminal gang hijacking his computer, which is why the police were there, expecting a known crime boss to collect the funds. Alex takes pride in his ability to deceive the deceiver, assuring James that his money is still secure and that he is not the man that they were or are looking for, expertly calming the storm of anger so that James discloses his new location as Antalya, and requests that the funds are redirected to there.

'He's in Antalya, Turkey,' Barry's voice bounces through the phone, vibrant and urgent in the stillness of the night.

I sit up, my heart racing as I awake from my slumber and his words register.

'I'll get a flight out there first thing tomorrow morning. Do you want to come with me?' Barry rushes the words out, barely pausing for breath.

'Are you serious? That sounds incredible! Yes, I'd love to join you!' Excitement bubbles inside me, spilling over in a grin.

'Perfect! There's a flight at 7 am. I'll pick you up early and fill you in on everything during the drive.' His enthusiasm is contagious, banishing any prospect of returning to sleep tonight.

As soon as I hang up, a jolt of excitement courses through me. It's midnight, but I jump from my bed and dive into the chaos of packing, clothes flying into my suitcase in a vibrant whirlwind. 'I need to be brave,' I whisper to myself, tossing in an extra pair of shoes, just in case. 'And ready for anything, especially what may or may not unfold with Barry.' My thoughts race alongside my hands, each item packed, fuelling a thrilling uncertainty, a bridge into the unknown. My heart beats wildly, alive with the tantalising possibilities of both closure and new beginnings. What awaits me feels just within reach, and I can hardly contain my anticipation.

After a sleepless night, a very early start, and quite a few hours spent travelling, I am exhausted, hungry, and relieved to be in Antalya with Barry and heading out for something to eat as the sun sinks low over the city and harbour, painting a shimmering orange stripe across the water. I luxuriate in the feeling of the warm, salty breeze as it caresses my skin.

I catch Barry's eye as we stroll along the quay. 'Can you believe how beautiful it is here? Far too beautiful to be hiding a scum bag,' I say, gesturing towards the horizon.

Barry grins, his sunglasses reflecting the glow of the sunset. 'This must be a good restaurant, as it is full of locals having fun,' he says. 'Shall we eat here?'

I turn my head to see a group of Turkish families laughing and sharing stories, their joy infectious. Clinking glasses and chatter spill out of the colourful terrace lined with tables, blending perfectly with the gentle lapping of waves against the harbour wall.

'Have you decided what you fancy to eat?' I ask, feeling my stomach rumble as we scan the menu.

Barry hugs me against his side, and I bask in his conspiratorial smile. 'It's our first surveillance trip together, so let's go big – how about those grilled prawns? They sound delicious.'

'Sounds perfect,' I reply, raising my glass again. 'To our first night of what we hope will be a very successful trip.' 'I'll drink to that!' he echoes, the clink of our glasses joining the party on this beautiful, warm evening. Barry looks pensive. 'Fingers crossed that James is still here. Apparently, he was spooked in Spain, so he may be very nervous and moving on frequently, although the team that followed him to here don't think that he knew he was being followed.'

'Yeah, he has to be here,' I reply, glancing at the boats dancing lightly on the water's surface. 'He's too arrogant to think we might be on his tail.'

A knot tightens in my stomach at the thought of facing him. I can feel the now-familiar surge of anxiety mixed with determination bubbling up. 'What if he's close? He'll recognise me if he sees me,' I whisper.

Barry's gaze flicks to the bar's entrance, his eyes sharp and scanning. 'If he is, we'll spot him before he sees us,' he reassures me, attempting a smile that doesn't quite reach his eyes. The worry lines on his forehead deepen as he drains his glass.

I grip the table edge, the plastic tablecloth crinkling under my fingers like the tension in the air. 'I want to confront him. I need him to face what he's done.' My voice is firm, but the tremor in my hands betrays my resolve.

Barry studies me, his expression serious. 'We have to be careful, alright? We can't rush into this. We don't know how he will react if cornered, and we don't want to compromise the police investigation.'

'I know,' I promise, though a flicker of doubt crosses my mind. Electric and unacknowledged tension lingers between us, but the urgency of finding James overshadows everything else.

'Let's walk around the harbour,' Barry suggests, glancing over the bustling restaurant one last time as he gestures for the bill, and we stand to leave.

'Okay,' I reply, pushing my sunglasses back up my nose. Despite the late hour, I feel more comfortable behind their disguise. I feel the weight of something heavy settle in my chest as I watch the waves shimmer and dance under the fading sun. I can almost forget the darkness that brought me here – almost.

As we step back onto the quayside again, the warm coastal breeze embraces us, yet the thrill falters. 'Do you think he's living nearby?' I whisper, gesturing towards the luxury apartments before us.

Barry nods, his jaw clenched as he glances toward the harbour. 'Yeah, he's probably renting one of those up-market holiday apartments by the water. I would, too, if I were living here. Our fraudster does love the finer things in life!'

My heart races at the thought of James lurking in the shadows, the unfinished conversations between us hanging like storm clouds above. 'Yes, from what I know of him, I would say that you're right,' I say, a mix of determination and dread coursing through me.

We begin walking along the waterfront, and I ponder the romance of the setting. However, the beauty surrounding me feels laced with sadness. 'It's lovely here,' I murmur, gazing up at the sky, yet inside, I'm restless, sensing a storm brewing.

'Aye,' he responds, his gaze sweeping across the horizon. 'But we must stay alert and be prepared for whatever lies ahead.'

I nod, feeling the bittersweet air cling to my skin like a lover's caress as we approach our hotel, the inviting cosiness of our separate rooms beckoning from the first floor. 'Tonight was nice,' Barry says, his voice low and laced with sincerity. He shifts his weight, his deep, understanding eyes locking onto mine, capturing the fading light with an intensity that sends a shiver down my spine.

'Yeah, it was,' I reply, my tone playful, yet my heart races with an unspoken promise of more.

He steps closer, the heat radiating from his body drawing me in, his gaze searching mine with a delicious curiosity. I can't help but smile, a spark flickering between us. 'Can I...?' He leans in, hesitating just a breath away, his warm breath mingling with mine.

I tip my head slightly, a spark of anticipation igniting, and softly whisper, 'Yes.'

His warm, salty lips graze against mine, sending a jolt of electricity that lingers in the air long after he pulls back, stuffing his hands into his pockets. The echo of our kiss hangs between us, filled with yearning and unfulfilled desire.

'What are you thinking?' he asks, his voice soft but probing, pressing against the weight of my uncertainty.

I take a deep breath, feeling the shadows of my past crowd in, the thrill of the moment entwined with a tangled ache. 'I think that was lovely, but we need to focus on catching and confronting James,' I confess, my voice barely above a whisper, masking the deeper emotions swirling within me.

Barry nods, understanding evident across his face. 'I get it. You have to close that chapter first.'

'It just feels complicated,' I admit, a frown creasing my forehead. 'You have been such a tower of strength to me and such a good friend, but...'

'But?' he prompts gently, crossing his arms, trying to shield himself from the unspoken hurt.

'I can't start something new until I let go of what's been,' I say, my throat tightening. 'You know?'

'Yeah,' he replies, and I can see a flicker of disappointment in his eyes. 'Just know I'm here. When you're ready.'

As he turns and leaves me at the threshold of my room, I feel both relief and sadness. This beautiful but unfinished moment hangs heavily around us like the darkness enveloping the outside world.

This morning, I am starving and shovel down my breakfast as if it might vanish off the plate. 'We need to get moving,' I say to Barry, my eyes darting to the clock as my heart races

LOVE, LIES AND BUTTERFLIES

with excitement and determination for my first full day of surveillance.

As we step onto the busy street, the chaos of the colourful weekly market in Harbour Square comes into view, and I can't help but grin at the mix of tourists and locals milling about. 'This is going to be like finding a needle in a haystack,' I joke, bewildered by the vibrant faces that stream past me. 'Do you think we blend in?' I ask, adjusting my sunglasses to sit just right. While I may not be able to mimic the locals, I can embrace my role as a tourist!

Barry chuckles softly, adjusting his shades. 'We should be fine. Just act natural.'

We finally settle on a table outside a charming coffee shop, the rich scent of roasted beans swirling with the warm breeze. My stomach flips – whether from nerves or the aroma, I can't tell. I look around, determined to study all the faces that drift past.

'This spot's perfect; we can see the whole street and most of the harbour,' I say, taking a tentative sip of the incredibly strong coffee before me and waiting for the bitterness to settle.

Barry nods, a smile creeping across his face. 'Being here together is kind of nice, isn't it?'

I return the smile, but it fades slightly. 'Yes, it is. If only we could find what we're looking for.'

We fall silent, my enthusiastic gaze systematically drifting from face to face. The air is heavy with unspoken thoughts.

'Do you ever think about what happens after?' I break the stillness, my voice barely a whisper.

'After? You mean once we finish this?' Barry's eyes narrow as he considers the question. As our eyes lock, a grin spreads across his face. 'Maybe we'll be the ones walking hand in hand and laughing next.'

It's mid-morning, and the sun is baking us, throwing harsh shadows on the cracked pavement. As we lean back in our uncomfortable plastic chairs, we observe the market and the streets emptying, the tourists heading for the beach, and the locals going about their daily routine. I squint at the desolate road ahead, frustration bubbling inside me. 'I can't believe we've been waiting here all morning, and he's not shown; it's market day, for Christ's sake, and even fraudsters need to eat!'

Barry sighs, brushing damp hair from his forehead. 'This heat is brutal,' he whines as he wipes sweat from his brow with a crumpled napkin and glances at the motorcycles zooming past. The engines roar like angry bees. 'All this noise is giving me a headache.' This is the first time I have recognised that Barry whines and moans a lot, but he is safe and loyal, and I guess no one will be perfect!

'Let's head over to the harbour,' I say, longing to be near the water. The calm might help us clear our heads. From there, we can regroup and determine our afternoon surveillance plan.

Barry nods, relief flickering across his face. 'Good idea.'

As we stroll toward the water, a desert breeze rustles the palm trees, offering temporary respite from the oppressive heat; the waves tickle the harbour walls, their soothing rhythm like a whispered promise.

Barry glances at the road, a frown tugging at his lips. 'James had better show up soon.'

'I really hope so,' I say, sensing his irritation. Hours have slipped by, and this isn't as much fun as I imagined.

Barry catches my eye, a grin creeping onto his face. 'Welcome to my world; surveillance is a real pain!'

We purchase some cans of Orangina and perch on a low wall, watching the sun glimmer on the water, enjoying its playful reflections. Suddenly, Barry nudges me, an edge of excitement in his voice. 'Look over there!'

I follow his gaze, and my breath catches. James stands tall and athletic, wrapped from head to toe in designer clothes that almost shimmer against the stark white harbour walls. 'He's like a misplaced model, and I probably have paid for some of that outfit,' I whisper, trying to keep my tone light.

'Right? Where's he headed?' Barry is now in full business mode.

James strides purposefully past the brightly coloured fishing boats with their tangle of mooring ropes and fishing nets, his long legs gliding toward the symphony of chiming masts on the gently swaying yachts at the far end of the harbour.

'Should we go after him and say hi?' My voice trembles slightly, a mix of nerves and nostalgia.

Barry shakes his head slowly. 'Let's just watch. He's heading to the yachts. Let's see if he boards one of them.'

I can't help but stare. I feel numb; there's something about him that feels... different now. But maybe it's just that my perspective has shifted.

Barry chuckles softly. 'Do you think he even knows how out of place he looks?'

'Maybe. He likes to think that he's richer, stronger, cleverer than the rest of us, so this look fits him perfectly!' I roll my eyes, the words laced with disdain.

James suddenly pauses. It's as though he can sense our eyes on him, and he turns back to scan the area before stepping onto one of the piers. Our eyes meet briefly, and I quickly look away, confident that my sunglasses will mask any spark of recognition. And it works; his long legs propel him onto the deck of one of the largest yachts in the harbour. My heart races when I read the boat's name magnified through Barry's camera phone lens: 'Deception'.

'Wow,' Barry murmurs. 'He's made himself right at home here, hasn't he?'

I can't suppress a smug smile. 'Yeah, and we will ensure everyone knows he's a fake in this world of fancy clothes and glittering yachts!'

Chapter Thirteen – Hidden in Plain Sight

Barry crouches beside me, his smirk growing more expansive in the sunlight. 'Can you believe this?' he whispers, his eyes glinting with mischief.

I shake my head, keeping my gaze fixated on the boat rocking gently on the water. 'I know. It's like he owns the place and revels in it,' I reply, barely able to tear my eyes away. On the deck, James leans back, swirling a glass of wine, completely at ease and unaware that he is being watched.

Barry lifts his phone's camera, the crisp click breaking the silence. 'Look at him. Just soaking up the sun,' he scoffs. 'All this time, he has been hiding in plain sight. And the name of his boat? It's almost a taunt to his victims.'

I nod, anger bubbling beneath the surface. 'It's sickening.'

Pulling my phone from my pocket, I unlock the screen, my heart racing as I type. 'Hey, Lucy! You won't believe what just happened!' I type, feeling the vibration of my excitement.

Watching the message form, I almost hear her voice: 'What is it? Tell me!'

Taking a deep breath, I squint at the blinking cursor. My fingers hover for a moment before I continue. 'We have found him, and I am watching him as I type this! I'll fill you in on all the details later.'

My chest tightens in anticipation as I hit send, the thrill of sharing this moment with her electrifying the air around me.

Barry squints, adjusting his grip on the camera. 'We need to gather as much information as possible about what he is doing before we hand anything over.' He leans slightly to get a better view; the tension in his shoulders is clearly evident.

I nod, heart pounding. 'It feels like we're in a movie. I can't believe we're doing this.'

'Shh!' Barry whispers harshly, his gaze locked on James, who thankfully remains oblivious to our presence.

I bite my lip to suppress a giggle. 'Sorry!'

I can't help but admire Barry Brown as he leans against a palm tree, casually examining the photographs he has captured of James, a confident grin playing on his lips.

James lounges on his boat, his fingers flying over his phone for what feels like an age, but then something shifts. He stands, stretching his arms overhead. The way he arches his back sends a thrill through me, a familiar feeling that awakens memories I'd rather forget. And then he leaps from the boat and strides toward us, his eyes fixed and determined.

'He's coming!' I glance at Barry, his gaze sharp and serious.

'Yeah, and we need to move – now!' Barry's urgent nod pulls my focus back, and tension brews between us. 'Let's go. We need to take cover and then follow him,' Barry says, his voice low but intense, a flicker of determination sparking in his gaze.

'Right behind you,' I reply, my heart quickening as we dart towards the darkness of the quayside supermarket.

To our horror, James follows us into the shop, the bell above the door jingling cheerfully to announce his arrival. He inhales deeply in the doorway, savouring the mix of fresh herbs and citrus.

'Hello, Mr James! The usual?' The shopkeeper leans against the counter, proud of his broken English and wearing a knowing smile as he reaches for a familiar bottle.

'Yeah, nothing beats a good red,' James replies, his fingers brushing over the label like an old friend's face. He holds the bottle up to the light, nodding with satisfaction and creating the illusion that he is a connoisseur of fine wines.

Barry and I stand in the corner of the shop dedicated to tourist trinkets, watching James approach the fish counter. A shiny skin catches James' eye, and his smile widens. 'There you are!' he exclaims, pointing at the fresh red snapper nestled among the ice. 'Perfect.'

'Mixing it up with a salad tonight?' the shopkeeper asks, already turning toward the salad bar.

'Absolutely. Give me some of that mixed salad, too,' James says, watching as the vibrant colours of a Mediterranean salad are carefully scooped into a plastic box.

The shopkeeper glances up as he finishes packing James' choices; his gaze darts toward us momentarily. James catches the look but thankfully dismisses it.

'Thanks for this!' James says, gathering his shopping.

'Enjoy your afternoon!' the shopkeeper calls after him as he turns to leave.

'I will do! You, too!' James replies, his voice drifting back as he steps out into the sunlight and strides back to his boat.

Hearing James' voice again sends shivers down my spine, and sensing this, Barry spontaneously hugs me, which is incredibly sweet of him.

'Look, he's not going anywhere today, so let's go and talk to the harbourmaster to see what he knows about the boat called Deception,' Barry suggests as he takes my hand, and we wander towards the official-looking government building at the head of Harbour Square.

As we approach, the harbourmaster emerges from his office, adjusting his cap. Barry quickens his pace.

'Excuse me! Sir!' Barry calls, weaving through the crowded quay.

The harbourmaster halts and turns to face him. 'Hello, Sir; how may I help you?' he asks, curiosity etched on his features.

'I'm an investigator and need some information about a boat here,' Barry replies, breathless. 'Can you help me?'

'Ah, what do you need?' the harbourmaster responds, leading us back inside his office.

Barry glances back at me, excitement dancing in his eyes. 'Could you please show me the registration details for the boat named Deception on pier 5, I believe?'

'Of course,' the harbourmaster says, flipping through a folder. 'Here we go.' He slides a document across the desk. 'The captain is a man called James Anderson. Here is a copy of his passport. He is also the registered owner of this boat and has paid four months' berthing fees in advance, all in cash.'

Barry leans closer, scanning the paper. 'No upcoming voyages planned?'

The harbourmaster shakes his head. 'Nothing filed. Just that payment last week.'

Barry's brow furrows as he processes this information, his mind racing as he photographs the document. 'Thanks, that's helpful!'

Once we're back outside, a familiar excitement buzzes in Barry's veins. 'We now know who he is!' he announces as he pulls out his phone and dials his police contact.

'Hey, it's Barry,' he says when the officer picks up. 'I've got a lead on our fraudster.'

'Yeah? What do you have?' The officer's sharp and attentive voice crackles through the line.

'His name is James Anderson,' Barry says, his gaze fixed on the yacht named Deception bobbing gently in the distance. 'He's on a yacht in Antalya harbour; I'll send you some pictures. I believe we'll find the tools of his trade onboard.'

I follow his eyes to where James lounges on the deck again, a glass of wine in one hand and a laptop open in front of him. The sunlight glints off the screen, and I can't help but feel a twinge of anxiety. Is he manipulating some poor, innocent woman who believes that he loves her, like I did?

'Okay, I'll contact our team in Antalya. We'll obtain a warrant and prepare the necessary manpower. This could be the break we need,' the police contact confirms.

Barry exhales, a wave of relief washing over his features. 'Thanks,' he replies, a hint of hope in his voice. 'I'll keep an eye on him until you get here.'

After the call, he takes my hand. His grip is firm, and I sense the weight of this moment between us. Words aren't necessary; our thoughts hang in the air unspoken. My inner turmoil stirs, but as I look at Barry, the anxiety starts to fade. Instead of resentment, I am grateful to James for leading me to this remarkable man.

The afternoon has turned into evening, and the cooler air envelops us as we stroll around the marina. The gentle lapping of the water against the boats provides a rhythmic beat. Barry's posture is relaxed, yet I can see the intensity in his gaze every time he looks towards the boat named Deception.

'Look at him,' he murmurs, nodding toward the dim light flickering from the yacht's cabin. 'He's in there, probably working his charm on some poor unsuspecting woman.'

I sigh softly, scanning the shadows that dance on the water's surface. 'You think he's got another victim lined up, or is he too busy covering his tracks?'

Barry smirks, his eyes narrowing. 'With James, it's always both. He loves the chase but is a master at slipping away when things get too hot to handle.'

As we move closer, the glow from the cabin becomes brighter. I glance at Barry, who suddenly adopts a serious demeanour. 'We can't let him play us for fools,' he says, his voice carrying a steely edge.

Barry tilts his head toward the cabin as we perch ourselves on a strategically placed wall for observation.

'We need to ensure he doesn't get the chance to destroy any evidence. I want to see him squirm.'

Confident that he is settled in for the night, we return to our hotel in the pretty harbour square as midnight strikes.

I swing open the door to my room, and without thinking, I lean into Barry. My heart races as our lips meet, a fleeting and unexpected connection that sends a jolt through me.

'Wow,' we both breathe, eyes wide, the air around us crackling with energy.

'Sorry, I –' I start, the words tumbling out.

'Don't apologise,' he replies, a grin on his face.

The corners of my mouth pull upward, and I can almost feel the electricity pulsing around us, dispelling the uncertainty that lingered moments before. Excitement bubbles just beneath the surface, bold and exhilarating.

We can now do nothing but wait for the team to be assembled to raid Deception. Time stretches but somehow keeps us caught between what is and what could be until the shrill ring of Barry's phone summons us back to our current reality.

'Hey, it's Sergeant Duval from the Fraud investigation unit, are you there?' An abrupt Mediterranean voice crackles through Barry's phone.

'Yes! What is happening?' Barry replies, urgency threading through his words.

'We're setting up the search now. Just stay put, we'll call you with the details as soon as possible, but it looks like early morning,' Sergeant Duval instructs, then hangs up.

The phone slips from Barry's grip and bounces onto the bedside table as he takes me in his arms and kisses me. Together, we stare out the hotel window towards the water, our hearts racing with anticipation on so many levels.

Chapter Fourteen – And So the Cards Tumble

It's sunrise, and I lean against a wooden railing as instructed by the police team, feeling the salty breeze whip through my hair. 'Can you believe this?' I say, barely able to contain the thrill bubbling inside me.

Barry shields his eyes from the early sun, squinting towards the gathering getting ready to board Deception.

My heart races. 'How do you think he will react?'

'Hard to say.' Barry shoves his hands deep into his pockets, glancing nervously at the uniformed officers bustling about. 'We just have to wait and see.' His eyes fix on the shadowy shape of the boat, tension radiating from him.

I force a grin, trying to lighten the heaviness between us. 'Just a couple of curious onlookers who were silly enough not to go to bed and be here at 6 am, right?'

'Right,' Barry answers, though his voice wavers. 'With a vested interest in the outcome,' he jokes.

Silence falls, the calm before the storm. The early morning sun warms us, yet a chill slithers up my spine as I wait coiled in anticipation.

The gathered team of police creeps around the sleek exterior of the yacht, their footsteps cushioned by the polished deck. A few exchange tense glances before suddenly converging and bursting through the cabin door, the hinges breaking free under the sudden force.

The door crashes open. Inside, James jolts upright from his dreamy semi-conscious state, eyes wide with surprise as the police team floods in, their torches and uniforms stark against the luxurious backdrop. The air is tense as the calm of his retreat shatters.

I lean closer, lowering my voice as if the air might carry James's name. 'Are we sure James is in there? He was so convincing, so... charming. If he is, this is such a relief.'

Barry nods decisively, 'No one will fall for his act anymore, my love. Today, the charade ends. He's not the king anymore.'

I squint toward Deception, its glossy surface betraying whispers of treachery. 'What will happen now?'

Barry leans back against the sturdy trunk of a palm tree, exhaling slowly as his breath mixes with the salty air. 'He'll face charges back in the UK. They won't take it lightly. He'll probably go to prison.'

A heavy sigh escapes my lips. 'I just want justice for all the women he has hurt and my money back.'

'That's exactly what you will get,' Barry insists, his intense gaze unwavering. 'I'm pretty certain that on that boat, we'll find evidence linking him to everything. It's all falling into place.'

Suddenly, a commotion interrupts us. I turn just as James, handcuffed and flanked by an officer, staggers onto the deck of Deception. The unkempt look, a far cry from the suave image he once held, washes over me like a torrent.

'Look at him,' I mutter. 'He's nothing without his designer clothes.' Bitterness seeps into my words. 'He looks like a different man.'

'That's the real him,' Barry replies, his eyes narrowing as he watches James. 'Beneath the façade, that's who he is.'

'Do you think...' I hesitate, my thoughts racing. 'Do you think he'll try to talk his way out of this?'

'Probably,' Barry scoffs, a dark undertone to his voice. 'He'll shout, make threats. That's his playbook.'

Right on cue, James's gaze meets mine as he is ushered into the waiting police car, and a flicker of malice ignites in his dark, menacing eyes as he recognises me. 'You have betrayed me!' he bellows, his voice reverberating against the harbour walls. 'You think I'll just roll over? You're making a mistake!'

A shiver runs through me, but I dig deep for strength, meeting his glare without flinching. 'No, James. You're the one who made the mistake.'

Barry shifts, placing his arm protectively around my shoulder. 'Let's get a cup of coffee,' he suggests, breaking the tension. 'The show is over for now!'

I divert my gaze as the police car swallows James. 'Yes, let's do that. Shame we can't have champagne; I want to savour this moment.'

As we walk towards the familiar harbourside café, a subtle buzz of excitement envelops me. A spark of hope ignites within – the past is behind me now, and the future feels like it's shifting, poised to bring something better my way.

The Hunter and his Prey

Barry's demeanour begins to crack, the corners of his mouth lifting ever so slightly as he feels a burgeoning warmth inside – a reflection of his connection with Jane and his respect for the other women ensnared by James's calculating charm. They are not just victims but seekers of love, much like himself.

As he watches James, now haggard and hollow-eyed, being escorted away by the police, a sense of triumph washes over him – a hunter finally seeing his prey ensnared in the trap he has patiently woven.

Hours trickle by until the call he is waiting for shakes Barry's phone to life. His heart races, and disbelief sweeps across his face. 'It's even better than I hoped!' His voice trembles excitedly, and he can't contain the energy coursing through him.

'Deception is a treasure trove,' he gushes, the words spilling out in a rush. 'They found the phones, a laptop, cash – all linked to the women I'm working for, and more.' He shakes his head, a smile breaking free. 'The boat's real name is 'Sunny Times.' He rented it in Spain and then vanished, leaving a mountain of unpaid debts. It's been masquerading under different names, just like him.'

The interrogation room is cold and stark as James sits across from the detectives, the harsh fluorescent lights overhead illuminating his anxious expressions. His gaze flickers around the sterile space, shifting like a cornered animal calculating its next move. There is a gnawing realisation deep within him – he is ensnared – yet instinct fights hard to claw back, to manipulate the narrative that has him trapped. The familiar dance of deception is still within reach, but the music has changed and is now discordant and unforgiving.

The police teams exchange glances loaded with conviction. James is a man trapped by his own web of fraud and theft. Yet, as they embark on lengthy deliberations over jurisdiction, the labyrinth of international crime and tangled responsibilities loom. Theft charges from Spain, deception and money laundering in Turkey, and romance fraud in the UK spin a complicated tale.

Finally, a decision is reached: James is to be deported and held in custody in the UK. Two burly British police officers prepare to usher James Anderson and heavy boxes of incriminating evidence back to his homeland.

His past will converge there, and his future reckoning is set to unfold.

'Mission accomplished!' I whisper, sinking into Barry's embrace as we ready ourselves to leave Turkey. The airport looms ahead, but this moment feels timeless.

'It most definitely is,' he replies, his lips brushing against mine. The kiss is warm and unhurried, signifying that we're entering new territory. Last night looms in my mind – the heat of our connection finally igniting between us.

I glance at him, his smile lighting up the room. 'This trip has been so much better than I expected,' I say, snuggling closer. 'Better than any time I had with James,' I admit, unexplainably feeling the need to stroke Barry's ego.

'Yeah? What's different?'

I search for the words. 'It just... feels right,' I finally say, a soft smile spreading across my face.

'Right is good,' he nods, his eyes sparkling. 'I'll take safety and love over lies and deception any day.'

At this moment, I know my heart is in good hands.

I barely focus as we settle into our seats on the flight back to the UK. The hum of the plane's air conditioning and the softness of Barry's hand should be soothing, but with James handcuffed to police officers and sitting a few rows behind, I can feel the burn of his stare.

'Hey, you okay?' Barry asks, his voice pulling me back to reality.

I force a smile, though I can feel my heart racing. 'Yeah, – mind wandering. It's strange, being on the same flight as him.'

Barry glances over his shoulder. 'I can see why that'd be unsettling. But he can't hurt you anymore. You know that, right?'

I nod, though I still feel fidgety. 'I know, but it's just... reminder after reminder, you know? It's like I'm trapped in a loop of embarrassment.'

Barry leans closer, lowering his voice. 'Forget about him. We've got plans to make, right, and friends and families to meet?'

I chuckle softly. 'I never had that with James. Weirdly, it was missing. Another facet that was so wrong, but I didn't see it.'

'You must stop berating yourself; be grateful that you're free of him, happy and healthy, and moving forward,' Barry says reassuringly. 'That's what matters. Let's focus on us. '

The heaviness in my chest lifts slightly as we talk. Barry is trying so hard, and I try to cling to the warmth of his words. But now and then, my gaze slips behind, where James's silhouette looms like a shadow over me physically and mentally.

Chapter Fifteen – Reflections and Ripples

It's been eighteen long months since our trip to Antalya, and the tension is palpable as I survey the courtroom with Barry by my side.

As the judge looks over the gathering before him, his expression is unreadable. 'Mr James Anderson,' he begins, directing his gaze toward the defendant, 'you stand accused of a series of elaborate and cruel frauds.'

James squirms in his seat, his fingers nervously playing with the cuff of his shirt, a stark reminder of his current circumstances – an M&S shirt and tie box set. It's not lost on me that it's precisely the sort of shirt and tie that Barry would wear, and it contrasts so sharply with the crisp, thick cotton of James's usual designer wardrobe. 'Your Honour,' he says, his voice steady but low, 'I didn't mean to deceive anyone. I was just... lost.'

The prosecutor leans forward, eyes narrowed. 'Lost? You defrauded numerous women across the UK! How is that being 'lost'?'

James looks up, meeting the prosecutor's piercing gaze. 'It was never my intention to hurt anyone,' he replies, his tone growing earnest. 'I only wanted to escape my reality. I channelled Robert – my twin. I have done so since he died when we were fourteen; he was always the boy, and the imagined man that I wanted to be,' he explains, his eyes clouding with an almost desperate vulnerability.

'Pathetic!' The prosecutor scoffs, crossing his arms. 'By using the excuse to yourself of channelling your dead brother, you've made a significant amount of money from romance fraud at the expense of many women.'

James's jaw tightens, but he holds the prosecutor's gaze, urgency flooding his voice. 'You don't understand. He is always in my head, motivating me to strive for more and be more like he would have been.'

The Defence Lawyer stands tall, his wig balanced with precision and his glasses sliding down the bridge of his nose as he strides toward the jurors. His voice is steady, his speech precise.

'Ladies and gentlemen,' he begins, his hands gesturing toward the seated figure of James, 'imagine a child navigating a world that feels hostile and confusing.' He pauses, letting the weight of his words settle in the room. 'James's childhood wasn't just difficult; it was a battleground marked by trauma.'

He steps closer, locking eyes with the jurors. 'James hears his dead brother's voice. He is mentally unwell and needs help. The collection of passports found in his possession are like pieces of a shattered mirror, each one affording him a different identity, a way to escape his torturous grief. Do you see that?' He points decisively. 'He wasn't just shifting roles; he was trying to keep his twin alive in his mind, to piece together a sense of self in a world that has fractured him.'

The murmurs among the jurors swell as he gestures to James. Condescension echoes in his voice. 'How could any of us understand the weight of that?'

A woman jolts from her seat in the gallery, her hands trembling. 'He is not mentally ill; he's a con man who lied and cheated! He bought me gifts and promised me a future!' Her voice rises, each word sharper than the last. 'But all he really did was steal my money!'

The room erupts in a chorus of voices. 'And me! He did the same to me!' another woman shouts, her fists clenched.

'Me too!' Another voice rings out, filled with fury, eyes blazing.

A cloud of evident outrage whirls above the assembled gathering. More women stand, voices chiming in, each carrying the weight of betrayal. Anger laces the tension.

James glances at the judge before turning to the women, his face a mix of despair and pleading. 'I never meant for it to go this far,' he says, his voice quaking. 'I loved you all... in my way. I just wanted to be someone else.'

The judge brings the courtroom to order, and an uncomfortable silence replaces the shouts; it feels like a collective holding of breath. He shifts his gaze over the restless gallery and then back to James, who slumps, defeated and pathetic. The judge clears his throat, slicing through the tension. 'We're going to take a brief recess,' he announces, his voice firm. His gavel is decisive in the hushed room as the audience spills into the hallway, following the scent of coffee and the clatter of plastic chairs in the canteen.

As Barry pushes the courthouse door open, the cool breeze hits us, and I shiver. 'Take a deep breath,' Barry reminds me, glancing back, his eyes filled with concern.

Lucy stands beside me, her hand resting lightly on my arm. 'It's okay, really. We're all in this together,' she reassures softly.

When I looked out at the rows of faces in the gallery, each one telling a story of hurt and betrayal, my throat felt tight. 'I thought I was one of a select few, not part of a conveyor belt of heartbreak,' I admit, my voice barely above a whisper.

Lucy squeezes my arm tighter. 'You're not alone. Look at all of us.' She gestures toward the others. 'We've all been through it.'

'Yeah, but...' I start, my gaze falling to the ground. 'Seeing them all lined up like that. I feel like... like I'm just one of many. It's as if we are all just nobodies.'

Barry steps closer, his voice firm but gentle. 'You are not a nobody. Your story matters. They may be victims too, but that doesn't detract from your experience.'

I look up at him, searching for comfort in his words, but doubt floods back. 'It's hard to believe that after what we have just witnessed.'

'Yeah, it's tough,' Lucy chimes in. 'But we're here to support each other. You can't let him win by feeling this way.'

We step outside, and the crisp November air bites at my cheeks as I huddle deeper into my coat, drawing the collar around my neck. The rustling leaves dance around my feet, swirling in the wind like a painter's brushstrokes. While I admire autumn's golden and crimson tapestry, a heavy weight settles in my limbs, dulling the joy that usually brightens this season. My breath forms small clouds, mingling with the chill, as I move slowly towards a strategically placed bench at the foot of the courtroom steps, each step a reminder of my fatigue.

'I'm surprised at how much this morning's proceedings have affected me,' I mumble, staring at my hands.

Barry inches closer, letting his warmth seep into my side as he touches my shoulder. 'Step by step, you've got us,' he says smoothly, his voice steady. 'You need to take this one day at a time.'

'I just don't get why I feel like this,' I admit, my gaze fixed on the ground.

'What do you mean?' Barry asks, concern etched on his face.

I close my eyes, and the memories of James flood back like a relentless tide. The weight in my chest tightens, and I feel a familiar ache. It's as if every joy I've ever felt is a fragile glass ornament – one wrong move, and it shatters. My hands tremble slightly, and I instinctively pull away from Barry. I don't want his affection at this moment.

'It's like I'm reliving all the pain,' I whisper, barely louder than a breath. As a sharp pain radiates through me, making my heart race, I stare down at my fingers, curling them into fists. What if I let myself feel hope, and it slips away again, leaving nothing but emptiness?

I shake my head, a bitter smile twisting my lips. 'I am a fool, and I don't deserve to be happy...' The bench's cold metal grounds me in this moment of uncertainty. It's safer this way – it's better to hide than risk being hurt again.

'Hey,' Barry interrupts. I can hear his frustration as he squeezes my shoulder gently. 'We're not going to let James do this to you. Do you hear me?'

'I know,' I whisper, a lump in my throat tightening. 'It feels like I'm drowning in all these thoughts.'

Barry tightens his grip, a reassuring presence at my side. 'Then let's park those thoughts for a bit. Let's focus on today; hopefully, you will never have to see him again. Is that okay?'

I nod slowly, enjoying the warmth of his presence around me, like a comforting blanket. 'You're right. Thank you, Barry; I don't want to lose sight of that.'

A soft smile spreads across his face, his eyes lighting up. 'You won't. We're in this together.'

As we return to our seats in the gallery, whispers ripple through the crowd, rising and falling like waves. James sinks deeper into his chair below us, the past creeping around him like a suffocating vine, which my imagination fantasises is poison ivy! I am sure he can feel the weight of our stares, judgment simmering beneath the surface.

The judge leans forward, locking eyes with the jury. 'You all have seen the evidence,' he says, his voice steady yet heavy with disappointment. 'You've heard from both sides. Now, you must sift through the tumult and determine the truth.

'Undoubtedly,' the Judge continues, his tone sharpening. 'This man, James Anderson, stands accused of living a lie. Using the name J XYZ, he seduces vulnerable women with false promises, charming them into believing in a future that will never exist.'

A deep breath fills the room as he presses on. 'But you have to decide. Did he manipulate their emotions, spinning tales of danger to extract money? Did he promise them love while plotting his escape with their savings?'

James's heart races, a mix of fear and defiance. He looks up, locking eyes with one of the jurors, desperation etched into his features. 'I'm sick. I never meant to hurt anyone!' he pleads, his voice barely above a whisper.

The judge continues, unwavering. 'Or is he merely a womaniser, a puppet in a game of love, where these women willingly offered their support, expecting nothing in return?'

The judge's gaze narrows. 'Your decision will shape this man's fate. Is it deceit or delusion? You must decide if James Anderson is the villain or simply the victim of his fantasies.' His gavel settles on the wood before him as he wraps up, leaving everyone contemplating the web of choices and consequences.

The jury is dismissed, and their deliberations begin.

Reflections – Jane

My fellow women and I sit rooted on the hard wooden bench of the courtroom gallery, our energy drained, each breath heavy with unspoken emotions. Today has been an emotional rollercoaster, much more challenging than I expected.

As the judge summarises the case, I gaze down at the man I once loved – the man I once believed was my soul mate. I remember the warmth in his eyes, the softness that cast a shadow over my heart. There, before me, sits the man with whom I shared dreams and secrets, but now I face the harsh reality that I ended up with the persona of his dead, and much less pleasant, brother, Robert.

My mind flashes to moments of betrayal – the lies that ripped through my life, the nights spent tossing and turning, fuelled by heartbreak. The image of him, once tender and loving, now feels like a cruel joke. It ties a knot in my stomach, and pity and anger swirl. The judge's voice echoes in my mind – vulnerable women, James is clearly disturbed, a man crushed by life's misfortunes. Yet, this does not excuse the wounds he's inflicted, not just on me but on countless others who have shared their painful truths today.

James is nothing but a fraud and a monster. A lousy memory – a chapter in my life that deserves to be closed and forgotten.

Reflections – James

As James sits in the dimly lit courtroom, the weight of uncertainty presses down on him. Shadows dance across his face, reflecting the turmoil within. He stares at his hands, palms sweaty, noting the smoothness of his skin that tells a story of a life of privilege. Memories flicker in his mind – faces of women he misled, their laughter replaced by disappointment. A lump forms in his throat as he thinks of his ex-wife Fiona and their daughter, whom he has not seen since the divorce, the imagined hurt in their eyes piercing through him like shards of glass when they become aware of what he has done. He can already imagine the whispers that will follow him, tarnishing the remnants of his reputation.

At that moment, a quiet resolve begins to stir within him. The thought of rebuilding the fragile bond with his daughter weaves into his heart. He envisions apologising, seeking help, and finally giving his brother's memory the respect it deserves. His parents' displeased looks hover in the back of his mind, a ghostly reminder of how far he has strayed from the values they instilled in him.

But just as quickly as that sentiment blossoms, it is overshadowed by another presence within him. The 'Robert' persona surges forth, a confident smirk curling the corners of his mouth. The thrill of the chase buzzes through his veins, drowning out the guilt that just threatened to surface. He leans back, folding his arms, a casual disregard sweeping over him. The courtroom feels like a game, and he is the master of the game. To him, his accusers aren't victims; they are jealous spectres, haunting him with their accusations. In his mind, he can hear the chorus of their anger, yet he stands firm, feeding off the adrenaline that comes with the danger. Robert feels invincible, a conductor of chaos, and the rush of control is intoxicating.

Reflections – The Judge and Jury

The courtroom buzzes with tension as the jury files back in, their faces a mixture of determination and exhaustion. The foreman stands, clearing his throat, while all eyes fixate on him.

'We find the defendant, James Anderson, guilty on all counts,' he declares. The words hang in the air, heavy and final. A ripple of applause sweeps through the gallery, where a group of women sit, their expressions a mix of relief and sorrow.

Hours later, the judge's voice rings out, steady and authoritative. 'James Anderson, this court sentences you to five years in custody.' He glances at the notes before him, his brow furrowing. 'While I recognise that part of you may seem harmless, it's clear that your twin persona – Robert – is dangerously manipulative.'

'You will undergo a full psychiatric assessment and, for at least the early part of your sentence, reside in a secure hospital and are instructed to undertake full assessments and any treatment that they deem necessary,' the judge continues, the gavel resting heavily in his hand.

A gasp escapes from the Gallery as the judge's following words resound. 'Any of your assets that can be liquidated will be sold to repay the women that you have defrauded. This includes the significant sum of cash found hidden on the boat.'

'Finally,' another woman breathes out, her eyes shining with unshed tears. 'We'll get our money back.'

The Judge nods in acknowledgement as he lists the debts to the yacht company and others, and the women exchange glances. This is their victory, but sadness, pity, and regret still settle over them.

'I didn't want to be part of this,' a smartly dressed woman of about fifty with dark curly hair murmurs, shaking her head. 'It's just a waste of everyone's life.'

'I know,' another replies softly, her eyes downcast. 'It's not a victory. It's just... the end of something we never wanted to begin with.'

The Judge looks at James, who hangs his head. His fate is sealed. He will lose his freedom, reputation, and the possessions that have come to define him as a man.

Chapter Sixteen – Too Much Too Soon

Time has passed since the trial, and I have gradually dealt with my demons and am starting to feel like myself again. Barry and I have settled into a routine that, perhaps on reflection, is too comfortable.

Barry is needy and can turn warm moments into suffocating ones. As I settle into the familiar rhythm of life with him, the weight of Barry's whining and expectations presses down on my shoulders.

The buzz of my friends has become an escape – a reminder of the independence I fought so hard to rebuild. But Barry watches closely as I enjoy my time with them, the subtle frown on his face betraying his hidden frustration. I almost hear the unspoken words: Why do you need them when you have me? I notice the flicker of resentment in his eyes whenever I mention an outing with my kids or a coffee date with friends. It's as if, in his world, my need for others is a puzzle he can't quite fit together.

Then, the argument comes crashing down like thunder on a clear day. I wander through the aisles of Sainsbury's, picking out groceries amid the chaos of a bank holiday crowd. My phone buzzes relentlessly. The worried tone in his voice strikes me like a jarring note in a melody that should be sweet.

'You've been gone ages; I was worried something happened,' Barry whines.

'I'm just buying groceries,' I reply, irritation creeping into my voice as I glance at the long line of fellow shoppers. 'It's a bank holiday. Everyone is out shopping!'

'You could have texted,' he counters, the lightness of his words masking an underlying tension I'm becoming all too familiar with.

'It's just Sainsbury's, Barry! You need to stop doing this!' I exclaim, barely containing my frustration, feeling the weight of each word as I hang up. The lingering silence of my phone is cut through moments later by a text that makes my blood boil: 'Drive carefully, I love you!'

With each flick of my thumb as I text a response, my heart races, feeling the tug-of-war between his affection and my desperate need to breathe.

Yesterday's argument highlighted a fundamental issue for me, but Barry has dismissed it as a 'tiff.' He behaves like nothing had happened as the morning sun spills over the small table where we sit in his cottage kitchen. He pours coffee into two mismatched mugs, the smell rich and inviting.

'Hey,' he says, flashing a smile that monopolises his features. 'What shall we do today?'

The coffee cup warms my hands as I stir. 'Maybe we could take a trip out and visit Sarah and the kids?'

His expression tightens, and a flicker of irritation crosses his face at the mention of my daughter and her family. I watch with irritation as he leans back slightly, arms crossed, and declares with a tinge of impatience, 'No, we should stay here and sort out the shed, and perhaps even paint it. It's about time we brought some life back into it!'

I catch him glancing out the window with a contented smile as he watches the birds flit about. 'I love this view,' he adds, oblivious to my feelings. 'It's peaceful here.' And then, without any warning, launches into the dreaded question: 'How would you feel about moving in with me permanently?'

I knew that this moment would come, but a weight has settled in my chest. Barry and his cottage wrap around me like an old, warm blanket – cosy, safe, and suffocating. Lately, everything has felt foreign. The walls are painted in vibrant hues, and knick-knacks line every shelf, a jumble of memories and stories that, no matter how hard I try, I can't see as anything other than clutter.

I reflect on my hard-won independence that Barry doesn't understand or respect and my sleek, modern, minimalist home, each corner meticulously curated. This house and this relationship reflect Barry and are poles apart from who I am and what I want.

The past two years with Barry have been a whirlwind; we have shared laughter, music, and new experiences. There were times when I felt alive, from the vibrant lights of concerts to the intimate whispers shared on rainy nights at the theatre. But now, with the James chapter firmly closed, the recent developments in our relationship linger in an unsettling shift in my heart.

I am suffocating. The warmth of the fire crackles softly, yet the silence between us feels weighty, as if the walls themselves are listening, waiting for my reply. Barry's gaze is steady, filled with a hopeful certainty that sends a chill down my spine. He speaks of plans and dreams, but as he outlines visions of a shared future, the room transforms into a cage that tightens around me.

My thoughts race – a whirlwind of yearning and dread. I can almost see the roots he imagines intertwining us, but all I can feel is a sense of displacement. The idea of moving here, of rearranging my life, and ultimately giving up my friends to fit into his picture-perfect scenario, gnaws at my insides. The quaint charm of the cottage, with its ivy-clad walls and rose-filled garden, once felt idyllic, but now looms over me like a heavy cloud.

I don't love Barry; I like him and feel safe with him. As I shift in my chair, the fabric clings to me. I picture mornings filled with sunlight, shared breakfast conversations, and the comfort of companionship. Yet, as quickly as the images form, they flee, replaced by visions of isolation in a place that is not mine. No matter how hard I try, I can't find a comfortable corner in this daydream, and the anticipation of living in a comfortable, safe, and predictable environment with him leaves me restless.

And just like that, I arrive at another crossroads in my life. I've put so much effort into finding me, creating my sanctuary, my home, which to me feels like a fortress. The thought of giving up my home and my independence for an uncertain life or another relationship that might crumble is a risk I cannot contemplate.

Barry, still oblivious to my unease, reaches across the table to take my hand. The touch that once sent a pleasant shiver up my arm now feels intrusive. 'I love you being here; please consider moving in. I am sorry if sometimes you find me a bit much, but we are made for each other.'

'I am just not ready,' I reply, finding the courage to continue and tell him how I am feeling. I lay my cards on the table, knowing that it could be the end or a more understanding beginning; I will never know until I do.

Barry squeezes my hand gently, but avoids looking at me. 'We're building something great, aren't we?' he says, his voice barely above a whisper. 'I see us living together, being a couple.'

I swallow hard, the weight of his words hanging between us. 'I care about you, Barry. You know that.'

'And I love you,' he replies, his sincerity cutting through the air. The table feels like an island, separating us. 'Don't you see the future we could have?'

I don't know where to look, so out of the window to watch the leaves dance in the breeze feels like a safe option as I say sadly, 'I am so grateful for you and everything that you have done for me, and I think that you are amazing, but I am so sorry; I just can't see us having a future together. I don't know what I am looking for, but I don't think it's this, and you deserve my honesty.'

'I am finally back on my feet emotionally and financially after James, and I want to take a moment to reflect on that. I am so sorry to have hurt you.'

He clenches his jaw, the hurt flickering in his eyes.

I add, trembling. 'I just need time to reclaim my life, to figure things out.'

'I understand,' he murmurs, but I can see the hurt etched in his features. As I leave, Barry turns to me, his brow furrowed.

'Are you really sure about this?' he asks, his voice barely above a whisper.

I force myself to breathe, the weight of his question settling in my chest. 'I have to be, Barry. I need to figure out who I am without us...' I repeat sadly.

He steps closer, arms outstretched, but I retreat from him, the distance becoming a wall I didn't want to build. 'I care about you. You know that,' he says, his voice cracking.

'I know,' I whisper, feeling the tears threaten to spill over. 'Maybe one day... we'll figure this out together.'

With a deep sigh, I collect my things and my car keys and then do hug him tight, savouring the warmth but feeling the space between us grow by the second. As I step back, the air feels chilly with unspoken words.

'Take care of yourself,' he murmurs, his gaze lingering on me a moment longer before he turns and walks away, leaving me with a heart full of guilt at hurting him and uncertainty about whether I have made the right decision.

The cosy cottage and investigator life bubble he will retreat to seem now so distant from the chaos in my head.

I have been home for a week now, and there has been no communication from Barry, but a chill runs down my spine as I step onto the porch this morning. There it is – a black bin bag full of my random possessions that had made their way to Barry's cottage during our relationship on the welcome mat. I lean closer, and my fingers tremble as I reach for the crumpled note tucked inside.

'I'm sorry,' it reads, the handwriting jagged and shaky. 'But having this around me is breaking my heart. I miss you so much x'

I can almost hear the voice that wrote it, choked with emotion. 'I'm so sorry that I've hurt you, Barry. It was just too much, too soon for me,' I whisper to myself, fighting back the tears. But eventually my chest constricts, and I bury my face in my hands.

I wipe my eyes with the back of my hand. Outside, the world feels too bright and cheerful for this sadness. A bird chirps nearby, oblivious to my turmoil, and I take a shaky breath.

'I'm sorry,' I say into the silence, hoping the wind carries my words. The sobs come in waves, crashing over me as I sit surrounded by remnants of what once was my relationship with Barry. The black bag is a heavy reminder of what, in time, I may or may not regret having so coldly tossed away.

Chapter Seventeen – Back to Square One.

I glance over at Sarah, my little girl transformed into a confident young woman, as she gently stirs her steaming cappuccino. The frothy milk dances in the cup, creating delicate, mesmerising patterns that swirl together. It's a comforting moment, one that fills me with gratitude. For the first time in a while, I can enjoy our time together without the weight of guilt over Barry hanging over my head. It's refreshing to feel this sense of freedom once more.

'Can you believe it's spring again?' she says, glancing at the blossoming trees lining the street outside the café. I notice a hint of nostalgia dancing in her voice.

I smile, looking at her. 'It feels like only yesterday that we were playing count the daffodils as we walked to the park when you were in the pushchair.'

She chuckles softly, her eyes twinkling. 'Time flies, doesn't it?'

'Faster than we'd like, but nothing can take our memories away.' I sip my lukewarm latte. The taste grounds me.

'Let's make sure to create many memories with my kids this spring,' Sarah suggests, her voice sincere.

'Absolutely. Let's start with a day out this weekend; I could do with some of my gorgeous grandchildren's special cuddles,' I reply, my enforced 'I'm doing just fine' bravado slipping momentarily.

'Deal!' she responds, her smile brightening even more. The coffee shop chatter blends with our laughter, reminding me how much I love my family.

My daughter beams. 'I am so lucky to have you, Mum.'

I glance outside as the sun filters through the trees, casting playful shadows on the ground. Life is good; life is for living, I reflect.

Sarah reaches for my hand, her fingers warm and gentle. 'What's going on, Mum? What happened with Barry?' Concern is evident on her pretty face.

I look up, catching her worried gaze. 'It didn't work out, and we split up,' I say quietly. 'You seem sad?' she asks, her tone softening.

I nod, letting out a shaky breath. 'It wasn't working for me, for many reasons, and I needed to move on. Perhaps I am just happier on my own now,' I reply. 'And so here I am, single, emotionally battered, and trying to pick up the pieces again.'

She leans in, her eyes searching mine. 'You've never told me what happened with James?'

My voice steadies. 'There was a time when I couldn't talk about... well, about James. I was so ashamed.' I pause, watching her nod as though she understands more than I realise. 'Now I feel detached; it's as if I am watching someone else's story unfold on one of those Netflix shows we used to binge-watch together,' I continue, a smile creeping onto my face.

She moves closer, her curiosity piqued. 'What changed?'

'I don't know,' I say, my heart racing, the warmth of the coffee coursing through me. 'Maybe it's the caffeine kicking in, or maybe it's just that I'm finally ready to tell the story.' A bitter chuckle slips from my lips. 'Let's just say he didn't just break my heart. He took everything – money, trust, hope.'

'I didn't know it was that bad,' Sarah whispers, her eyes wide.

'Oh, yes; it was that bad and worse. But I learned a lot and managed to get my money back,' I assure her, hoping to lighten the mood. I shake my head, frustration creeping in. 'I thought I was ready for something real with Barry, but I wasn't. His love was suffocating. I hurt him, Sarah. Really hurt him.

'Maybe I lost myself in both relationships,' I admit, my voice barely above a whisper. 'I was so naive with James and believed his lies, allowing him to manipulate me. And with Barry? He was safe and loyal, and he made me feel better after everything with James. However, I couldn't see myself with him forever, and I wasn't honest with him or myself about that. I was the fraud this time.'

Sarah bites her lip, her brow furrowing as she thinks. 'No, Mum. You could never be a fraud. He wanted more than you could give right now. So... what now? What do YOU want?'

I shrug, fingers tracing the rim of my cup as I peer into the milky liquid. 'I just want to find myself again,' I say, my voice barely above a whisper. 'I want to learn to love without losing who I am.'

'Then let's start here,' Sarah replies, her smile radiating warmth that seeps into the chill around us. 'Make today the first day of your new chapter. One step at a time.'

My smile ignites a flicker of self-belief. 'When did you get to be so wise?' I ask softly. 'Maybe this time... I can rewrite my story.'

Sarah sips her coffee, her eyes sparkling with encouragement. 'You've got this.' She threw her arms around me. 'You've been through so much, and look at you now.'

I glance around the cosy café, the light filtering through the window, casting its glow on everything. 'I do have a lot,' I admit, feeling a surge of strength. 'My health, my home, my job, my family...' I trail off, memories swirling – laughter, support, the mistakes scattered amongst the good times. 'They've always been there.'

'Exactly.' Sarah nods, her eyes steady. 'You have been there for all of us and have a whole support network behind you. It's time to focus on you.'

I chuckle softly, the tension easing from my shoulders. 'You know, this morning with you has planted a seed in my mind.' I stir my coffee absentmindedly. 'What if I write my story? Share my journey, embrace the therapy of writing it down?'

'Now that's a brilliant idea!' Sarah exclaims, her excitement contagious. 'So many women would relate to that. It's real; it's raw.'

A wave of pride washes over me. 'I'm a mother, a grandmother, and I have and will mess up. But those mistakes? They're my battle scars. I should be proud of them.'

'Absolutely,' Sarah grins, raising her mug. 'Here's to your journey. Let's see where it takes you!'

I lift my refilled mug of coffee in salute. 'To my literary adventure,' I say, savouring the taste as hope and excitement bubble in my brain.

Anxious to set the wheels of my adventure in motion, I drain my mug and embrace my daughter. As we step outside the café, the cool breeze is a gentle tonic that fills my heart with possibility.

At the local stationers, the scent of fresh paper greets me as I wander down the aisles.

My fingers glide over the notepads until I find one that feels just right. I then head home, my mind racing with ideas.

Settled in my sleek, modern sitting room, I cradle another cup of coffee. The pen hovers over the notepad, and the words come tumbling out. 'This is it,' I whisper to myself, the narrative of my life spilling onto the page. Each stroke feels like a release, as purpose and clarity take shape with every word that seeks its order in my timeline.

Recounting my story in a way that engages readers has become a passion project that consumes every spare minute of every day; if I am not writing, I am thinking about words, scenarios, and emotions. I am fortunate that the mere act of tapping a pencil against a blank page unleashes a torrent of words, ideas, and previously half-finished thoughts.

'I can't believe you're doing this,' Sarah says during one of her frequent visits, leaning against the doorframe, arms crossed. Her eyes shimmer with curiosity.

'Of course I am!' I reply, a grin breaking across my face. 'The beginning and the middle are solid, but the end. That's where the adventure starts.' I scribble a few words, then pause, tapping my pencil against my chin. 'It could twist in so many directions.'

Sarah raises an eyebrow, stepping further into the room. 'So, what's the plan?'

I lean back in my chair, the thrill of possibility sparking in my chest. 'That's the exciting part! I have choices. Each decision I make shapes how it all wraps up.' I gesture at the chaotic mess of words before me, my heart racing at the thought. 'Every plot twist, every character moment – it's all in my hands.'

'Just don't forget to leave room for surprises,' she says, a small smile tugging at her lips. 'You never know what might inspire you next.'

'Exactly! That's what keeps it alive.' I nod, conviction igniting my spirit. 'The ending isn't written yet, which allows me to truly enjoy the journey.'

Sarah chuckles, rolling her eyes. 'You and your dramatic flair. Just don't get too carried away. I'm eager to see where it goes.'

'So am I,' I reply, reinvigorated. As I pick up my pencil again, the page feels like a canvas waiting for me to fill it with stories of love, lies, and butterflies.

Chapter Eighteen – 'Jolie Retraite'

As I flip open the notepad, the familiar smell of its thick cream paper greets me. I glance at the corner where my scribbles peek out like shy little seedlings.

'Hey.' Sarah leans against my desk, a teasing smile on her face. 'How is your epic adventure coming along?'

I smile and tap my fingers on the pages. 'You wouldn't believe how much there is to explore. Each character feels like...'

'Like what?' she prompts.

'Like it's alive. It's like they are taking on a life of their own, growing and reaching for something.' I pause, staring at the blinking cursor on my laptop. 'Last night, I had a wild idea about where the story could go next.'

'Spill it,' she says, her eyes sparkling with curiosity.

'What if I rent a villa in Provence for the summer and attend a writing school there? I have the money back from James to cover the costs, and I love that part of France so much. I'm sure that the vibrant colours and fragrances, along with my newfound independence, will elevate my writing to a whole new level – one that challenges me as a writer and everything my readers will think that they know about me.'

'That may be just what you need, but will you be okay doing this alone, Mum?' Sarah says, wrapping me in a concerned hug.

I smile, closing my eyes as the image forms. 'I'm not sure, but I need an adventure, and this could be perfect.'

'Sounds like you're about to take your readers on a wild ride,' she says, playfully nudging me. 'Just don't enjoy yourself so much that you forget to write it down or invite us out to stay with you!'

I can feel the roots of excitement growing inside me, reaching out and ready to sprout new ideas.

Later that day, as I scroll through my emails, I pause, my breath catching, as I see the rental confirmation for 'Jolie Retraite', a beautiful villa just outside Avignon. 'Oh my goodness! I've done it!' I squeal, practically jumping out of my chair.

'Done what?' Sarah asks as I call her with my news.

'I've rented the villa and signed up for that writing course in Avignon!' I can hardly contain my excitement.

'No way! That's amazing! Where is the villa?'

'The course is in a gorgeous chateau!' I gesture animatedly with my hands. 'And the villa has a pool in a small hamlet nearby, mine for a whole month. It's all so perfect!'

'Wow! You're living the dream! When do you leave?'

'In a week,' I say, practically vibrating with enthusiasm. 'I can't believe it's happening. I can already see myself sipping drinks by the pool and writing with fields of lavender and sunflowers as the backdrop.'

'You're going to have the best time. I can't wait to hear all about it!'

'I promise I'll send you updates.' I grin, picturing the sun-soaked days ahead.

As I pack my final items for France, I pause over a photo of Barry and me. We were smiling, his arm protectively around my shoulders. I remembered how safe that had felt after James – how I'd needed that security.

But I also remember the suffocation that followed, the feeling of being wrapped too tightly in someone else's expectations. With James, I'd given away my financial security. With Barry, I'd nearly sacrificed my independence.

I place the photo in a drawer rather than the suitcase. This trip is about finding the middle ground – being strong enough to stand alone but open enough to let others in on my terms. The woman who'd desperately wired money to Turkey is gone. As is the woman who'd fled from Barry's suffocating love. Who is emerging now? I'm not entirely sure, but I'm eager to find out.

After a week of preparation and reservations, today has finally come. The breeze sweeps across a bustling Portsmouth harbour, carrying the salty scent of the sea. I shift my weight, glancing at the ferry looming ahead, its hull gleaming under the afternoon sun.

Have I got everything? I question as I peer into my car, filled with bags and gear. I hope I packed enough. But if not, I have allowed myself three days to navigate from the top of France to the bottom, so I can pick up supplies en route if I need anything.

Come on, you're going to be okay, I reassure myself.

Adjusting my sunglasses, I stand tall, my shoulders squared to the bright sun overhead. The warm breeze brushes against my skin, and I take a deep breath, trying to calm the flutter in my stomach. My fingers drum lightly against the railing, a silent rhythm betraying the bravado I wear like armour. The vibrant chatter around me is a backdrop for my racing thoughts – a collage of street signs and winding roads murkily painted in my mind. What if I take the wrong turn and get hopelessly lost? The thought sends a shiver down my spine, but I lift my chin higher, forcing a confident smile as I prepare to check in.

If you get lost, you'll get found! You're not alone – there are signs, and you have a satnav and your phone, right? I chastise myself, but my stomach still churns with uncertainty.

Taking a deep breath, I look at the horizon where the sea meets the sky. 'Epic, huh? Here's hoping.' And as the ferry horn blasts to announce its departure, I feel a surge of adrenaline. 'Let's do this,' I say to the seagulls that swamp us. With one last look back at England disappearing behind me, I set off, ready to embrace my next chapter.

France

The sun glistens across the dark tarmac of the open road as I grip the steering wheel tightly. My hands are sweaty, but a smile spreads across my face. The engine harmonises with my heartbeat; each mile I travel is a defiant anthem to freedom.

The road unfurls ahead, a smooth asphalt ribbon cutting through the French countryside. Regiments of vines stripe the hillsides. Golden sunflowers sway gently in the breeze, their faces turning eagerly toward the sun. Quaint gites and farms dot the landscape, each a charming haven with tidy gardens and welcoming signs. The air carries the warm scent of fresh pastries and the laughter of locals who fill the village squares, mingling with distant church bells. 'Why do overseas church bells always sound more exotic than the ones at home?' I question.

As I drive through little towns and villages, vibrant markets spring to life. Stalls burst with a riot of colours – crimson tomatoes, golden squash, and bright green cucumbers – all artfully stacked against the backdrop of weathered cobblestones and red canopies. I can't resist stopping and wandering through the maze of vendors; I love the sweet scent of ripe peaches mingling with the crisp aroma of fresh herbs, which fills the air with an enchanting bouquet. And how children's laughter partners the warmth of the sun to bathe the scene in summer vibes. Each bite of a juicy fruit tastes like summer, and I could quite easily stay here and lose track of time, enveloped in this soothing tapestry of French sights and sounds.

Back on the road, I feel invincible as memories of past loves echo, the voices of those who said I couldn't do anything like this. But their words only fuel my resolve. I laugh aloud, the sound mingling with the rushing wind streaming through the open window. Each second feels electric, a vivid reminder that I am carving my path. I focus intently on the beauty around me, relishing the thrill of this journey as it unfolds. The world is vast and inviting, and I am here to embrace it all, starting with all things French.

After three amazing days on the road, I pull into the crisp gravel driveway of my villa, 'Jolie Retraite', and the scene before me takes my breath away. The turquoise water of the pool glimmers, creating a shimmering dance that reflects the vibrant pink and red blooms dotting the compact garden. The rustic charm of the villa invites me in like an old friend.

I swing open the heavy wooden door, and soft, shuttered darkness welcomes me as a warm breeze sweeps past, carrying the sweet scent of the flowers arranged on a three-legged table in the hallway. The blooming jasmine spills over the door frame, framing the sun-drenched terrace outside. I can't help but smile as I whisper, 'This is perfect.'

The pool beckons me after the long drive; I rummage through my bag, my fingers brushing against the soft silk of my swimsuit. Sliding it on, the cool fabric feels like a gentle caress against my clammy skin as I step out onto the quirky, crazy-paved terrace. The warm, rough stones tickle my bare feet, and without a second thought, I leap into the aquamarine waters and luxuriate in the refreshing splash of a jubilant, icy embrace that sweeps over me.

As I float, the villa's garden takes on a stillness, and the sun's golden warmth touches my body while the cool water refreshes my skin, creating a delightful contrast that sharpens my senses. Each ripple of the water sends a thrill through me, and I can't help but smile.

After an afternoon of rejuvenation, I scan my surroundings, grounding myself. Tomorrow at 10 am, my course begins, and I feel a pull toward its location. A quick look at Google Maps reveals it's just a few miles away, sparking my curiosity to check it out.

As I drive into the nearby town of Avignon, the sweet aroma of freshly baked bread once again wafts through the air, this time emerging from a charming terrace of shops that tempt me to make a stop. I resist the urge, keeping my focus sharp.

Château Anaïs, the venue for my course, unfolds before me. Its beautiful architecture, perched by the river and overlooking the town, makes it easy to spot.

A glance at my watch reminds me that time has slipped away. I also need to buy supplies for this evening. Up ahead, a local supermarket glows warmly against the dusk – a beacon drawing me in. The excitement of discovering new foods mingles with the scent of fresh produce and the chatter of evening shoppers as I wander through the aisles, happily gathering what I need.

With my bags in hand, I retreat to the villa, prepare dinner, and settle onto the terrace with a glass of local wine for the evening, allowing myself the time to enjoy the wonder of nature as the sunset paints the sky above me.

Chapter Nineteen – Château Anaïs Day One

The charming bedroom of the villa is bathed in glorious early morning sunlight. Stripes of warmth criss-cross the crisp, white iron bed, where the delicate Broderie Anglaise bedding invites me to linger. I sink deeper into the cool cotton, letting the thrill of today's adventure pulse through me like a gentle current.

Barefoot, I glide across the cool stone floor, the texture of the stone refreshing against my skin. As I enter the rich, dark wood kitchen, the rustic French doors coax me to fling them open and take my coffee outside to the terrace, where I sit at the sky-blue-painted table, its legs wobbly yet welcoming, beside the shimmering pool.

The air is alive with a delightful fragrance, accompanied by a sweet symphony of birdsong. Butterflies dance gracefully around the carefully arranged shrubs and colourful flowerpots, adding a touch of magic to the scene. I close my eyes and inhale deeply, letting the vibrancy of the moment envelop me. A sense of wonder washes over me as I reflect on the day that lies ahead, filled with endless possibilities.

The pool beckons, shimmering like a thousand scattered diamonds, each ripple transforming into a miniature star. I stand at the edge, basking in the warmth of the morning sun as it embraces my skin. With a deep, exhilarating breath, I dive into the crystal-clear water. The coolness envelopes me, sending a delightful tingle racing across my body, awakening every nerve with a rush of invigorating energy.

As I break the surface and emerge, droplets cascade off me like jewels, and I shake my hair playfully, sending arcs of sparkling water dancing through the air. Standing on the villa's charming, slightly worn terrace, I wrap myself in a soft towel, taking a moment to acknowledge how, in this moment, my heart and spirit overflow with an overwhelming sense of calm and contentment.

Serenity surrounds me, filling my mind with creative energy, and I am ready for the course ahead. And so, with a sense of purpose, I rummage through my clothes, searching for the perfect outfit. I decide on a short linen skirt and a flowy summer blouse. The mirror reflects my choice – a look of effortless chic, just the vibe I aim for.

To complete the look, I adorn my head with a wide-brimmed straw hat, a charming accessory that shields me from the sun and exudes a carefree spirit. Slipping my feet into comfortable flat sandals, I grab my large straw bag. Its earthy colours remind me of the charming market on the drive down here, where I found it. I place my laptop, pen, and notebook inside, ready to embrace the day.

As I approach Château Anaïs, its towering spires pierce the sky, casting long shadows across the gravel drive. Each crunch beneath my tyres is a rhythmic welcome that seems to whisper secrets of the past. The ornate stonework, bathed in golden sunlight, sparkles like jewels, and ivy clings to the walls like a lover's embrace. A gentle breeze rustles the leaves of ancient trees, their branches swaying gracefully as if to beckon me closer. My heart races with anticipation, and I feel a magnetic pull towards the magnificent building, which promises a day of enchantment.

As I enter the hallway, the dark wood panelling contrasts sharply with the light stone walls, creating an imposing atmosphere. A petite, smartly dressed receptionist greets me in well-rehearsed English with a warm smile. She leads me to a room adorned with bistro-style tables and chairs. The Château is hosting several events and courses, and the soft chatter of my fellow students fills the air. Once inside, I am introduced to Ruth, the tutor for my course, who welcomes me with her smooth West Country accent as the receptionist gestures to a waitress colleague to fetch me a mug of coffee.

The Creative Writing course's table buzzes with quiet chatter and the rustle of paper. I scan the group, noting the eager expressions and scattered notes. Ruth, who in many ways bears a striking resemblance to an older version of Lucy, dominates the introductions; her hair is pulled back into a tidy bun, with a few silver strands glimmering in the warm lighting of the room. She wears a bright, daffodil-yellow cardigan, its vibrant yet inviting colour reminiscent of the Provençal sunshine.

To Ruth's side is a carefully arranged stack of books, all bearing her name, leaving us no doubt that she is both a talented and successful writer. I recall the evenings at home in the days before I left for France when I was immersed in her stories, with the vivid characters and gripping plots lingering in my mind long after the final page. There's a palpable respect in the air, an unspoken acknowledgement of her skill that draws our attention like moths to a flame.

The atmosphere shifts as we move from the dining room to our study base, a large room adorned with portraits of well-to-do French nobility watching our every move. It's immaculately presented, and presumably, priceless ornaments catch the light and glimmer in the substantial display cabinets that line the walls. A long rectangular table stretches down the centre of the room, dressed in thick green felt and perfectly set with water bottles and glasses lined up at each seat. The vast leaded windows are flung open along one side of the room, framing a stunning view of the grounds and blurring the line between inside and out, connecting us with the world beyond.

I slide into my seat next to a man who has been introduced to me as Pierre. His wild grey hair dances slightly in the soft breeze, each strand alive with its own story. The frayed edges of his double denim outfit cling to him like a familiar embrace. Yet, there was an undeniable air of nobility and intrigue about him – something that draws the eye to him.

I hesitate momentarily, unsure how to breach the unspoken barrier, but he takes his cue and leans closer, his vibrant blue eyes sparkling with mischief and warmth. The corners of his mouth turn into a smile that feels like an invitation, a promise of untold adventures. Deep lines carved into his face speak of years filled with joy and sorrow, and as he began to speak, the shadows seem to lift, revealing a passion that radiates from him like sunlight breaking through clouds.

His soft, eloquent voice flows like wine, rich and intoxicating, each word pulling me deeper into a world woven with love, loss, and the bittersweet taste of life. I quickly find myself eager to immerse myself in the tapestry of his experiences and uncover the treasures hidden within his tales.

Marjorie sits beside him, her round face free of makeup and framed by wild, tangled curls that catch the light with hints of silver. She wears flowing garments and multiple bangles that jingle and flutter around her as she speaks. A crystal pendant glimmers at her throat. Her hands arc gracefully through the air, and her bangles chime as she shares her thoughts on forest energies and the nurturing spirit of Mother Earth.

But the moment the conversation shifts to publishing contracts, something stirs within her. 'My agent secured me fifteen per cent on foreign rights last time,' she declares, her voice transforming, crisp and authoritative. She retrieves a sleek smartphone from her pocket with a fluid motion, her fingers expertly navigating a spreadsheet app, jotting down notes with brisk precision.

I blink, stunned. The woman who seemed to float in a flower power dream is now a commanding industry figure. The contrast is striking; Marjorie embodies the unexpected harmony of wisdom and business acumen, draped in an earth mother façade that beautifully conceals her formidable spirit.

Sitting beside her, David is like a spectre, his tall, slender frame and pale skin drawing light into themselves, casting an almost ghostly shadow amongst us. The furrows on his brow tell stories of burdens carried in silence, sharply contrasting with Marjorie's bubbly laughter that punctuates the air. He gazes at the half-empty cup before him, steam curling upward like the fleeting thoughts that slip through his fingers, caught between the roles of psychiatrist and dream analyst. A flicker of curiosity stirs within me – what would he see in my own dreams? An involuntary shiver runs through me, a warning to tread lightly.

The gentle tap of his fingers against the wooden table punctuates the murmurs around us. As he introduces himself, I catch glimpses of an older father, slightly dazed, as though the vibrant chaos of young children has left him reeling. Each tap resonates like a silent plea for clarity amidst the chaotic symphony of parenting. I observe him closely as the rhythm shifts – it becomes a murmur of longing, an echo of stories yearning for an outlet, moments of solace that remain tantalisingly just out of reach.

David sinks deeper into himself, the world around him fading into a blur. His grip on reality loosens as he wrestles with the storms within, lost in the tempest of thoughts swirling just beneath the surface. The desperation for escape hangs in the air in that heavy silence, a silent battle between the weight of his responsibilities and the elusive peace he craves.

As the door swings open, Robin bursts into the room with the force of a storm, a tall, lanky silhouette that calls to mind a scruffy Harry Potter lost in a sea of ordinary. His mismatched clothes hang loosely on his frame, the fabric dancing around him like a flag. Dark, greasy hair tumbles over his forehead, while patches of skin are dappled and uneven, telling tales of severe acne.

He rushes to his seat, the backpack swinging at his side, when suddenly – clatter! The water bottle escapes his grasp, tipping and releasing a flood of liquid that rushes like a wild river over his laptop. Time slows; his eyes widen, a look of pure horror etching across his face. The notepad – neatly positioned on the table in front of each of us as a receptacle for thoughts and jottings – for Robin is now a soggy canvas.

Around him, whispers of annoyance flicker through the air, but I can't ignore the raw panic in his expression. In that instant, my irritation fades, replaced by a bittersweet understanding. Robin doesn't just navigate the room; he manoeuvres through a world that rarely stops to consider the brilliance tangled within his chaos, a vibrant contrast to the facade of calm we project around him.

Carol's next as I assess my fellow students. Her hot pink nails shimmer in the light as she gestures animatedly, the flawless contours of her makeup enhancing her lively expressions. Her elegantly coifed white hair catches the gentle glow, framing her face with sophistication. At seventy-five, she moves with a grace that belies her age, a lively spark in her eye that draws everyone in. Her attire, a delightful mix of comfort and whimsy, makes the room feel warmer and more inviting.

As she speaks of weaving humour into storytelling, her laughter dances like music through the air, floating and twirling, filling every nook of the space with infectious fun. Excitement bubbles in me as I relish spending time with her, eager to share in this vibrant energy.

And then there is me, a young-at-heart middle-aged woman on a deeply personal journey of rediscovery and bucket list fulfilment. Filled with a whirlwind of ideas and driven by an insatiable desire to learn the art of crafting a compelling narrative that resonates, my path is not just about exploration but about transforming experiences into stories that inspire and engage.

The energy around the table brims with potential, each of us a vibrant thread in the tapestry of stories waiting to unfold.

Ruth stands at the front of the room, her eyes sparkling with enthusiasm as she engages the group. She grabs a whiteboard and scribbles our dreams and passions on it, weaving them into a vibrant narrative for the course. The energy in the room buzzes; laughter erupts, and nods of agreement ripple through us.

Glances dart around; shy smiles blossom as stories flow, aspirations blending like colours on a painter's palette. The unknowns that felt daunting just moments ago dissolve, replaced by laughter and a sense of determination. With every word Ruth speaks, our connection deepens as we embrace that we are a crucial part of the story we are creating together.

Our first challenge unfolds as we gather around the table. We are to create a short article about the large orange resting before us like a treasure. Marjorie, a seasoned artist with a penchant for the dramatic, leans forward, her fingers tracing the dimpled skin gently. Her eyes dance with a spark that lights up her face. 'Can you believe how perfect that orange is?' she breathes, her voice filled with wonder.

David inches closer, his excitement palpable. 'It looks like joy in a physical form!' he exclaims, and a wave of agreement ripples through the room, infecting us all with a contagious spirit of delight.

Ruth moves gracefully, her hands animatedly weaving through the air as she speaks. 'Think of the emotions you want to convey! Let the colours and the texture resonate with your feelings, for example: "The vibrant orange, glistening softly under the antique ceiling light, pulses with life. I take a deep breath, the sweet, citrus scent wrapping around me like a warm embrace, flooding my senses."'

'You know, I never really thought about how an orange makes me feel,' I say, glancing at Carol. Her eyes slowly widen as if a light bulb has flickered to life.

'You're right. I hadn't either. But now I see – sunshine. Fresh, beautiful, delicious!'

Her words paint vivid images; I can almost see golden rays spilling forth, cascading over the fruit. The thought of the bright juice inside bursts like the laughter of children on a sun-drenched afternoon. It's a taste of joy, a sweet memory of lazy garden days and carefree moments that tug at my heart with a familiar warmth.

The second exercise set feels like a solitary journey, a stark departure from our previous group dynamics. When Ruth announces, 'I want you all to write a scene from the perspective of someone who has hurt you or let you down,' my heart drops. James? Gavin? The thought of stepping into their minds feels like a burden I am not ready to bear.

Sensing my hesitation, Ruth reassures us, 'This isn't about forgiving them. It's about understanding the why. Sometimes, when we write these perspectives, we reclaim our power.'

I stare at my blank laptop screen, wrestling with a daunting emptiness. Then, as if the floodgates have opened, words crash onto the screen, raw and unfiltered.

'I never meant to hurt her. That's the lie I tell myself. But deep down, I crave the power. Something shifts inside me when she looks at me with those trusting eyes and hands over the money. I feel powerful and emboldened.'

With each sentence, I wrestle with the hidden demons that I thought I had left behind. I am no longer merely recounting my story; I am unearthing the layers of fear and resentment I've kept buried for so long. By the time I reach the closing lines, tears stream down my face – not from agony, but from the release of emotions that have for so long festered like a wound that would not quite heal properly.

As I finish writing and close my laptop, I feel lighter, like I have exorcised a phantom from my narrative.

Ruth's feedback on this narrative during my appraisal strikes a powerful chord, illuminating the vital importance of embracing other perspectives. This insight enriches the depth and authenticity of my characters and profoundly enhances my journey of reinvention. It's a reminder that true growth often stems from understanding the lives and experiences of others.

As the day unfolds, I feel the energy manifesting – ideas swirling in the air, igniting something within me. When the final words of the session are spoken, I pack my things with a deep sense of satisfaction that thrums in my chest, a feeling of accomplishment, reflection and fulfilment.

Driving back to Jolie Retraite, I glance up at the sky, its stunning blue background dotted with soft, fluffy clouds – a scene that makes me smile. 'I can't wait to sit by the pool and write this evening,' I whisper, a grin widening across my face. Images and emotions swirl in my mind, and my plan to incorporate the feelings and understanding of others' narrative perspectives into my story begins to take shape.

Chapter Twenty – Château Anaïs Day Two

It's 9.45 on our second day of the creative writing course; as I settle into my chair at one of the gingham-dressed round tables in Château Anaïs café, a freshly brewed pot of coffee and a plate of delicate pastries welcome me. I glance over at Carol, who beams, her eyes dancing enthusiastically as she takes a dainty sip of her Earl Grey tea.

'Did you do any writing last night?' Her voice carries an infectious energy, urging me to share.

I can't help but smile, a rush of pride swelling in my chest. 'Yes,' I say, my words spilling out with excitement. 'I spent time on the villa's terrace, absorbing the atmosphere. Each element – the blooming flowers, the rustic sandstone, and the rustling leaves – I let my characters' true personalities speak to me. My understanding of them and my senses were inspired, and I can't wait to share my writing with everyone today.' My fingers drum lightly on the table, a manifestation of my eagerness.

Sitting across from us, Pierre chuckles as he tears off a piece of his flaky croissant. 'You both get so excited about your work.'

And we share a chuckle, our laughter weaving through the cheerful chatter and the gentle clinking of dishes.

Carol springs to her feet with a dramatic flair, her notebook perched under her arm like a prized possession. 'Let's go! The study room won't wait for us!'

Her enthusiasm ignites the group, and we all scoot back our chairs with a chorus of scraping against the flagstone floor.

We ascend the impressively wide, red carpet-clad oak staircase. Our footsteps pulse in sync as each step propels us towards our study room for another creative day. The walls, lined with photographs and shelves of books, blur past in a rush, mirroring our eagerness.

Ruth glides into the room, her vibrant ensemble a kaleidoscope of clashing colours. 'Good morning, everyone!' she sings, her voice bright and brimming with energy. She stops at the head of the table, hands on her hips, her gaze sweeping over the gathering of eager faces.

'Are you ready to tackle another day?'

A few heads bob up and down while murmurs of agreement float through the air.

A grin bursts across her face, as radiant as her mismatched outfit. 'Did you all have your coffee? I was gentle with you yesterday, but trust me, copious amounts of caffeine will be a must today,' she adds, arching an eyebrow at Robin and David, who are struggling to shake off their morning drowsiness.

'Not yet, I overslept!' Robin groans quietly, rubbing the remnants of sleep from his eyes.

Ruth's laughter, bright and infectious, fills the room. 'Well, let's fix that first! You're on coffee duty! Any orders, please, to Robin!' The table erupts with a burst of chatter, each voice vying to place their caffeine requests.

'Today, we will learn about showing rather than telling.'

We discuss how to paint a picture with words rather than tell the reader.

Then, the group exercise involves taking the following text – 'Mia watched Jake walk into the house on a hot, sunny day' – and applying our newfound skills as a collective effort to transform the narrative into an impressive, show-don't-tell extravaganza.

'Wow, it's scorching out here!'

Jake squinted at the sun, his hand shielding his eyes as he stepped onto the porch. The wooden boards creaked underfoot, a familiar sound that echoed in the still afternoon air. He wiped the sweat from his brow, feeling the heat cling to him like a warm blanket. 'Are you coming in or what?' he called over his shoulder, glancing back at Mia, still standing at the yard's edge, her hair dancing in the summer breeze.

'Just a second! I want to catch my breath,' she replied, fanning herself. The vibrant flowers bordering the entrance swayed gently as if in rhythm with their conversation.

Jake chuckled, pushing open the heavy door. It swung wide with a creak, and he paused on the threshold. 'It's cooler in here! I think the air conditioning finally kicked in.'

'Lucky you,' Mia said, finally stepping inside. The blast of cool air met her like a refreshing wave. She could almost feel the heat evaporating from her skin. 'Maybe we should just stay inside all day!'

'Great idea!' Jake grinned, dropping his bag onto the floor with a soft thud. 'Who wants to be outside when it feels like a

sauna?' The two of them exchanged a knowing smile, stepping deeper into the cool embrace of the house and leaving the sweltering sun behind.

As I stare at our work, excitement bubbles inside me like soda fizzing in a glass. 'You know,' I say, glancing over at Carol, who is scribbling furiously, 'there's something magical about painting with words. It's like we're brushing colours across the canvas of the reader's mind.'

She looks up, her eyes sparkling. 'Exactly! It's like we can build entire worlds just with our descriptions!'

I smile, tapping my pencil against the paper. 'I can't wait for our breakout time. Can you imagine bringing all this to life in our own stories? I want to capture every detail, every emotion.'

'Same!' Pierre grins. 'Then we get to share it with Ruth and the group for critiques. I hope they are kind and see the vision I'm trying to create.'

I nod, my heart racing at the thought. 'I'm going to make it vivid. I want you all to feel like you're part of my story.'

'Right, team. This is excellent, very creative!' Ruth laughs, breathless with excitement, as she calls to silence the chatter. 'Now, let's revisit your work and paint the picture in our minds with your words!'

As I open my laptop and review the first chapter of my story through a 'show, don't tell' lens, I feel a rush, knowing this is just the beginning of how I will elevate my storytelling to a whole new level.

We huddle around our laptops until the late afternoon sun casts a warm glow over the table. Ideas swirl, filling the air with the soft hum of creativity. It's magical, and we all appear reluctant to break the spell that envelops us.

As the grand clock in the hallway outside our study room strikes 5 pm, Ruth leans back in her chair, a thoughtful smile spreading across her face. 'I don't know about you all, but I want to head out for dinner this evening. How about we make our way to my favourite bar in Avignon?'

'Sounds perfect!' Pierre's eyes spark with enthusiasm. 'I love the vibe there.'

'Yes! Let's escape,' David chimes in, lifting his glasses and placing them precariously on top of his head. His yearning for fresh air and a glass of wine is evident in his tone.

With a chorus of agreement, we rise and leave behind the elegant confines of the study room. As we step outside, a playful breeze dances around us, carrying the sweet scent of freshly cut grass, invigorating and fresh. We load our precious stories and writing paraphernalia into our cars with laughter and anticipation before embarking on our short walk into Avignon.

As we navigate the cobbled streets, the aroma of cooking wafts through the air, mingling with the distant laughter that spills from lively bars, each adding their own layer to the gorgeous summer evening. As we round a corner, the main square opens up, its expansive soft grey stone paving warmed by the late afternoon sun. Grand buildings loom like silent guardians, their timeless grace enveloping us.

'Over there!' Ruth waves her arms towards a charming bistro. Its enormous red and white striped canopy is a colourful and welcome respite from the still warm sun, shading its collection of randomly placed round tables.

'Perfect spot,' Carol agrees, her arms swinging by her side and footsteps quickening as she marches toward it.

The waiter approaches with a warm smile as we cosy up to the charming, albeit slightly worn, table. He gracefully carries a complimentary tray of freshly made lemonade in icy, chilled glasses that sparkle in the golden light. We excitedly grab our drinks, feeling the refreshing coolness as we offer, 'Cheers!'

Laughter erupts, filling the space like a lively orchestra. Stories flow like the drinks – each anecdote painting vivid images, from the tang of citrus on our tongues to the heartwarming tales that draw us closer together. The lively chatter forms a tapestry, weaving our voices in a vibrant melody that dances above the ambient sounds of the square. Shadows play on the cobblestones, and the glow of hanging lanterns casts a warm embrace around our gathering as we immerse ourselves in this moment of genuine connection.

Hours pass, food is enjoyed, and the drinks become alcoholic as conversations ebb and flow. Friendships deepen with each shared joke and story.

However, as the sun sinks behind the buildings, so does our energy, and the mental exertions of the day, coupled with a lovely, relaxing evening, envelop me in a soft warmth as I weave my way home through the winding lanes. Each turn is a whisper of familiarity that pulls me closer to the villa. Memories flutter in my mind like delicate leaves caught in a gentle breeze; laughter rings out, mingling with the vibrant chaos of crowded Turkish marketplaces. Barry and I, weaving through throngs of locals, our voices lost in the symphony of haggles and chatter.

Bright shades of spices and richly patterned textiles dance in my memory, yet an undercurrent of sadness stirs within, like a bittersweet cocktail that leaves a hollow ache in my chest. The road ahead twists and turns, and I feel the familiar grip of the steering wheel beneath my palms tighten as I pull myself back to the present.

A sudden jolt of adrenaline surges through me as I realise my speed. The approaching bend is looming larger than life. My heart races, each beat amplifying the tension as I lean into the turn. The tyres skid briefly on the dusty road surface, a reminder of the thin line between control and chaos. Time seems to stretch, and I feel a rush of vulnerability in that momentary pause. Then, with a sigh of relief, I emerge from the bend unscathed and am welcomed by the sight of Jolie Retraite unfurling before me, its terracotta roof bathed in the warm, amber glow of the late evening sun.

I arrive home and fling open the shutters and doors that lead onto the terrace. A thrill courses through me at the thought of a swim. And once again, I revel in the luxury of the cool water as my skin glides through it. Each stroke offers a release from the day's mental exertion.

Or so I think – but as I find myself in the coolness of my bedroom, a soft, white sanctuary waiting to embrace me, the world outside fades, and my mind ignites. Thoughts swirl around – vivid scenarios and characters vibrantly dance behind my eyelids. Ideas pulse with energy, each begging for attention, and the quiet of the night becomes my canvas.

Words spill onto the page of my bedside notepad, crafting connections and narratives that weave together seamlessly. Time slips unnoticed, and as the clock ticks closer to midnight, I drop my pen. The ink on the pad is still wet with my thoughts as I finally surrender to the pull of sleep, letting the day's inspiration fade into a backdrop of dreams.

Chapter Twenty-One – Living the Dream

It's another beautiful, sunny day in the Provençal countryside, with the sun's warm rays bathing the vibrant lavender fields as they sway gently in the breeze. I sit on my terrace, my laptop perched on its weathered wooden table, the smell of fresh croissants wafting through the air as I sip my café au lait.

It's not long before I find myself conversing with my laptop as I sit with my fingers poised over the keys. 'I have to capture this moment; it's like the perfect scene for my novel. Right! Middle-aged woman, divorced, looking for the real woman in the mirror, and despite taking many wrong turns on her journey, she finds herself living in a beautiful French villa.' Raising an eyebrow and aware of a smirk creeping across my face, I reaffirm, 'My debut novel is a bestseller waiting to happen!' I laugh, and then impostor syndrome looms its head: 'But all you talk about is her boring life.'

'Hey! Jane's life is anything but boring!' I retort playfully, feeling the fire of creativity ignite within me. I recall the jumbled feelings that inspire my characters, the emotional baggage of heartbreak and hope that form the backbone of my story. 'It's layered, like a good croissant – flaky yet substantial!' I declare, inspired by the last bite of my breakfast.

'Okay, fair point,' I remonstrate to the mug of steaming coffee, 'don't forget to add a dashing stranger who makes your heart race, but this time doesn't break it! Hmm. That's a chapter yet to be experienced and painted into my canvas of words, but I am forever hopeful!'

'Now you're talking! Make sure he's got a mysterious past, too!' A smile is by now tugging at my lips as I gaze at my surroundings and remind myself, 'You are living the dream, girl, so be proud!' I turn back to my laptop, my heart racing with anticipation as the cicadas begin their symphony, providing the perfect soundtrack for my unfolding tale. Each keystroke brings me closer to unveiling the secrets of my imagination, laced with the triumphs and trials waiting to burst forth from my soul.

The pages of my worn notebook crinkle softly as I flip through them, the ink of past musings still fresh in my memory. Sunlight spills across the table, and with each line I type, echoes of yesterday pierce through the calm. A sudden jolt catches me off guard – a forgotten argument, a betrayal that stings anew. My fingers hesitate over the keys, but I press on, letting the sadness swell around me, and then move on.

I can feel the sharpness of the words tumbling out, raw and jagged, as they find their place on the screen. My characters emerge, their struggles mirroring my own and more, each heartbeat laced with tension. As I write, I paint their pain in vivid strokes – the heavy sighs, the clenched fists, the restless nights – transforming my chaos into their stories, breathing life into their anguish. They rise from the depths of my memories, each crafted with aching authenticity, as if they were always waiting to be freed.

Time flies, and words flow effortlessly until the sun's position tells me it's mid-afternoon. I lean back, breathless, and stare at the screen as the word count clicks to 5,000. A surge of pride swells within me; tomorrow, at the Chateau, I will have the chance to share a piece of my soul and explain how my new skills have helped me craft it into a raw, honest, and hopefully page-turning narrative for the group to critique.

I realise that I have been so engrossed in my writing that I have hardly moved from the laptop all day, and my back is stiff. A tightness creeps around my body as rivulets of sweat trickle down my brow. Each keystroke now grows laboured, my sweaty fingers struggling against the slick surface of the keys.

Across the terrace, the pool shimmers, its surface dancing in the sunlight, calling to me like a siren. My throat tightens, dry and scratchy, while a gnawing hunger rumbles deep inside. But the lure of the water is too strong to resist; I can almost feel its cool, soothing embrace, which is both invigorating and refreshing. With a resolute breath, I push the laptop aside, my heart quickening as I stride toward the inviting blue water, pull my strappy sundress over my head, dive in, and luxuriate in the sweet relief of a swim.

With each length, my thoughts clear, and a sense of rejuvenation pulses through me. The faint scent of chlorine mingles with the fresh air, igniting a spark of freedom and wanderlust. I consider how I shall spend the rest of the day, and I can almost taste the romance of Avignon as it beckons me,

LOVE, LIES AND BUTTERFLIES

its cobblestone streets, charming cafes, and upmarket shops all inviting me to explore.

And so, an hour later, I wander into the bistro I have chosen from the many that frame the old square in Avignon. The sound of laughter and clinking glasses greets me like a friend. The air buzzes with energy, bouncing off the bold red and yellow walls. Twinkling lights that hang from above cast a soft glow, dancing on the polished wood tables.

As I settle into my seat, my fingers brush against the delicate wine glass, its cool surface a familiar comfort as I glance around. Couples lean in close, their laughter smooth and refreshing like the wine filling my glass. I catch fragments of their conversations – a playful tease here, a shared secret there – each snippet weaving into the lively tapestry of the evening.

I practice French in my mind, trying to piece together the melodies of the voices that flit through the air like butterflies. With each laugh that rings out, I can't help but feel the warmth of the scene enveloping me, even as I sit alone, feeling a little self-conscious.

'Hey, are you okay?' A voice breaks my thoughts, drawing my gaze to a friendly waitress whose command of English immediately puts my French to shame. Her smile is genuine and as bright as the evening sun.

'I'm good, just people-watching,' I reply, lifting my chin slightly, trying to match her warmth.

She nods, glancing toward the crowded bar. 'It's lively tonight!'

As she moves away, I take a deep breath, letting the world swirl around me. The couple at the next table clink their glasses, laughter spilling over their jokes. I could tune into their conversation, but instead, I focus on how I am feeling in this moment: calm, as the gentle breeze brushes against my skin, inspired by the soft glow of fairy lights twinkling like stars above me, and liberated as I stroke the cold surface of my glass – no longer a shield, but now a companion.

A gentle voice drifts past my table. 'What a lovely evening it is.' An older woman walks by, and I nod in agreement.

'Yes, it is,' I reply, grateful for a spark of connection, however fleeting.

As the square darkens and shadows descend, I lean back in my chair, soaking in the ambience – each sound and scene a reminder that I am not alone, but part of a vibrant tapestry of Avignon this evening. For the first time in a while, I feel a sense of pride swell within me, and I raise my glass, draining it as I toast to the night and the independent, interesting, sophisticated woman I feel myself becoming.

Raising my hand, I catch the eye of the waitress, who approaches with a friendly nod.

'Could I please get the bill?'

'Are you leaving already?' she asks.

'Yes, sadly. I have a busy day tomorrow.' I smile.

'Okay. Have a lovely rest of the evening.' She smiles as the machine in her hand spits out my credit card receipt.

'I will. Thank you!' I respond, putting ten euros under the ashtray for a tip.

'My focus has never been stronger. It's time to be the woman and author I know I can be,' I tell myself under my breath as I weave through the tables and out onto the street, back towards my car, my mind already drifting towards the tranquillity of my beautiful villa.

Chapter Twenty-Two - The Court of the Pen

The study room hums with low chatter. The rich, warm colours of the walls once again welcome the sunlight spilling through the large windows and casting gentle patterns on the long table around which we sit surrounded by papers and laptops, each a view into our hard work.

Ruth stands at the front, her presence grounding as she surveys our eager faces. A smile softens her features, and her voice flows like a soft breeze. 'I'm so proud of each of you,' she begins, her eyes twinkling sincerely. 'Sharing your work opens your soul to us all, so let's be mindful of that as we listen and offer honest yet kind feedback.'

Pierre fidgets with his notes, a nervous laugh escaping him. His fingers tap against the table. 'What if she hates it?' he whispers, looking around like the walls might have ears.

Carol leans closer, giving him a reassuring nudge. 'Don't even think that. This is your moment!' Her bright and infectious smile dispels some of the tension in the air.

I swallow hard, feeling the weight of the words and characters I have carefully committed to my story. My heart pounds a little too loudly, and I can sense the anticipation building in my throat. 'It's just that... this is our chance to be seen and appreciated,' I confess, my voice wavering like a delicate thread.

'Yes!' Margorie interjects, her hands animatedly clasped together. 'We poured our hearts into this. It's important to us!' Her declaration ripples through the room, igniting the spark of determination in our eyes.

Sensing the energy and nerves, Ruth raises her hand, and the room hushes. 'Remember, what you've created matters, regardless of any feedback you may receive today,' she assures us, a warm smile gracing her lips as she encourages us to approach the day as an opportunity to develop our narration skills.

Carol's Story - A humorous observation of life in the village in which she lives.

The village sprang to life as the sun peeked over the thatched roofs, bathing the cobblestone streets in a golden hue. Mrs. Thompson's floral apron, dusted with flour, beamed at passersby from her bakery's doorway. The warm, yeasty aroma of freshly baked bread enveloped the lane as children dashed by clutching flaky pastries like cherished prizes, their laughter mingling with the scent.

At the opposite end of the street, Mr. Jenkins, the grumpy old butcher, lounged in his doorway, arms folded, a frown etched across his face. Yet, as young Timmy marched past, clutching a stick sword, Jenkins couldn't help but chuckle at the boy's proclamation. 'I'll be a knight when I grow up!'

'Well, you'll need a bigger sword than that butter knife!' Mr. Jenkins retorted, the corners of his mouth twitching upwards.

Meandering further, I passed narrow shops, each a tale in its own right. Mrs Blithe, the eccentric florist, wove her hands through colourful bouquets, turning each arrangement into a living artwork. 'They're not just flowers, dearie; they're a bit of joy for the soul!' she called out, her laughter bubbling up like a sparkling brook as she weaved through the lane.

Near the village square, the pub buzzed with life. Clinking glasses and hearty laughter spilt out, inviting newcomers to witness the warm camaraderie. Faces lit up with stories shared in the flickering candlelight while the air danced with the comforting scents of ale and roasted nuts.

We all enjoy Carol's story; each character adds a vibrant thread to the lively tapestry of village life, making it impossible not to be captivated.

Pierre's Story – An Emotional journal about how he survived the Boxing Day tsunami but lost his family.

Pierre's smile fades as he rises, the warm glow of the room dimming in contrast to the weight of his words. He inhales deeply, his gaze drifting to the window, where the memory of a sun-soaked beach flickers in his mind.

He takes a deep breath, steadying himself as he looks around the room, his gaze meeting each pair of eyes.

'It was supposed to be paradise,' he begins, the calm of his voice contrasting sharply with the tremor in his hands as he recounts that Boxing Day. The sun's warmth seems to fade, replaced by shadows that flicker in his memory. His voice, a vessel for his pain, carries us through his emotional journey, from the initial shock to the enduring grief.

'Joyful laughter,' he murmurs, his voice catching, 'turned to chaos instantly.' A shiver runs through the air, and silence

LOVE, LIES AND BUTTERFLIES

wraps around us like a heavy blanket. We lean in, breathless, as he recalls when the ocean surged, wild and unstoppable. He grips the edge of the table, knuckles white, haunted by his wife's desperate cry for help, a sound that echoed over the tumultuous waves and the crushing weight of loss that followed.

His eyes glisten, betraying the storm brewing within. He recalls his daughter's tiny hand slipping from his grasp as he tried to save her and how it's etched into his memory like a photograph fading in the sunlight.

The audience sits in rapt attention, absorbed in the vivid recollections painting the scene before us, each detail brought forth in sharp relief.

He leans back, the weight of his words settling heavily in the room. Our stunned silence trespasses on his grief, and in that moment, we find a thread woven with strands of hope and healing, held together by the strength of his tale. Our empathy for his loss is overwhelming.

Robin - Embraces his passion for Science Fiction

'So, um, the robots... they, uh, they took over, right?' His voice wobbles as he reaches the climax of his thought. He pauses, glancing down, his cheeks flushing as the words fizzle in the air.

'Yeah, um, so the robots started making all the rules,' Robin stammers, forcing an uneasy laugh. 'Bizarre, right?' His confidence wavers, but he presses on. 'I mean, who knew a toaster could... you know, become a dictator?'

A snicker erupts cruelly from David, who leans back, arms crossed. 'Next thing you know, my vacuum will demand a pay rise!' The comment sends a wave of laughter through us, all our amusement echoing in the room and adding to the already awkward situation.

Ruth cuts in, reminding us that we are there to support each other, rather than mock, as Robin winces but tries to regain his footing.

'Right! I mean, can you imagine? A toaster making rules about, um, toast?' His voice squeaks slightly, but he rushes onward.

'It was supposed to be a metaphor! About, uh, society and – '

'Yeah, sounds like a real 'slice' of life!' Pierre whispers beside me, his tone dripping with sarcasm.

Robin is awkward reading his work to us, his cheeks burn red, and his whole demeanour flustered. As he stumbles over his notes, the pages slip and tumble like his thoughts.

'So, moving on to... um, the moral of the story?' he manages, his voice dropping to a whisper.

'It's about technology and... uh, the dangers, I guess?'

'More like the dangers of not preparing yourself properly to present your story!' Carol mutters, her voice low yet cutting, which is instantly rebuffed by a look of reprimand from Ruth.

With a defeated sigh, Robin's shoulders slump.

'Well, you get the idea, right?'

His voice is barely audible, the words drifting away like autumn leaves caught in a breeze.

The story crashes and burns, but I feel for him as Ruth steps in and supports his struggles to regain his composure among the remnants of his faltering presentation.

Marjorie shifts in her seat, her brows furrowed. 'What's happening here?' she whispers to David, who shrugs, perplexed.

'Darkness for the sake of darkness doesn't work for me,' he mutters. I can't help but nod in agreement.

Finally, it's my turn. I swallow hard, feeling the prick of sweat at my temples as I clear my throat. The shuffling of chairs ceases; a palpable hush blankets the room, drawing everyone's attention like moths to a flame. I take a deep breath, steadying my shaking hands, and begin to read the recrafted introduction to my story. Each word flows from me, carrying the weight of loss and heartbreak, yet woven through it all is a thread of resilience and adventure.

As I glance up, I catch Ruth's gaze – her eyes shine with curiosity, sparking like stars. When I finish, the silence hangs briefly before it shatters with her enthusiastic applause. 'That was brilliant!' she exclaims, her voice slicing through the tension in the air.

A rush of warmth floods my cheeks. 'Really?' I can hardly contain the surprise in my voice, an elated smile breaking free. My heart swells, feeling lighter than it has in ages. 'Thanks, that means a lot!'

Marjorie – has chosen to write about her passion for the Blue Vanda orchid

And bursts from her seat, her excitement radiating like sunlight.

'You guys are going to love this!' she declares, brandishing a vibrant picture of an exotic plant. The image boasts vivid blue petals that seem to dance on the page.

Ruth leans in, curiosity etched across her face. 'What is that?' she asks, her eyes narrowing as she takes in the details.

'It's called a blue vanda orchid,' Marjorie says, her eyes shimmering with enthusiasm. 'Isn't it stunning?'

'It looks lovely,' I say, a slight doubt tugging at my lips. The beauty of the flower is undeniable, but I can't ignore the nagging question. 'What's so special about it?'

For a moment, Marjorie's confident demeanour wavers.

'Well, uh... it has these amazing flowers,' she stammers, her voice quieter now. 'But it also grows in really unique places.' Marjorie scans the room as if searching for a lifeline, her gaze flitting from one person to another.

'Okay,' she says, her voice resolute once more. 'What if I tell you it has a fascinating pollination process? The way the insects interact with it is truly amazing!'

'Now that's the kind of hook we need!' Ruth chimes in supportively, her posture turning playful.

Marjorie takes a deep breath, her confidence returning like the tide.

'Exactly! Let me tell you all about it...'

David's - Literary interpretation of his Case Book

After what feels like an eternity under the spell of Marjorie's Blue Vanda Orchid, we find ourselves at the mercy of David's case book. As he reads, the air crackles with uncertainty, and I catch Ruth's eye. Her brow is furrowed in deep thought, her pen tapping nervously on her pad, mirroring our collective anticipation about his presentation.

'Do you know what an 'epistemological framework' is?' David's narrative questions.

We collectively shake our heads. As David enlightens us, 'It's how we know what we know.'

'It sounds like something out of a sci-fi novel.' Robin sighs distractedly, flipping the page of his notebook.

The way David explains the concept makes us feel as though we are being transported to a distant, incomprehensible world. He looks up, amusement flickering in his eyes. 'I sense some of you are not staying with me. Surely, it's not too challenging for you all to understand?'

Ruth opens her mouth to respond but hesitates, glancing at the notes scattered before us. 'It's just... a bit complex, that's all,' she finally says, attempting to keep her tone light and positive.

'Complexity is merely a challenge for those with simpler educational backgrounds,' David announces pompously, a smirk playing at the corners of his lips. His words hang heavy with condescension, and I can see Ruth's shoulders droop in dismay.

'You'll come to appreciate the nuances in time.'

By now, the group is becoming frustrated and irritated. The weight of the complex discussion is bearing down on us.

'It's not that we don't want to understand,' I add quickly, my voice barely rising above a whisper. 'It's just... a lot to take in.'

David leans back, his expression unchanging, as if the breadth of his knowledge were an impenetrable wall. 'Perhaps it's time to elevate those perspectives,' he says, fingers drumming lightly on the table, leaving us bemused and scrambling to grasp the heights his words have just scaled.

It's been a long and exhausting day, and Ruth sits upright in her chair. 'I have to hand it to you,' she says, her tone proud as she surveys the room. 'Your critique of each other's work today has been honest, fair, and spot on, and has also demonstrated that whilst we all write in different styles and genres, we must never forget that what one reader loves, another will not love.

There is no right or wrong in the narration; what is essential is that your work is well-crafted and well-written, no matter what the subject."

Chapter Twenty-Three – This Writing Life

Once again, I awake to the sun painting delicate patterns across my room. And once again, I wake up with a clear sense of purpose, a surge of energy propelling me forward. Today marks the beginning of a ten-day period dedicated to nurturing our creativity at home. Our goal is to use the skills that we have learnt to refine our novels and prepare them for Ruth's final evaluation and feedback. The appreciation Ruth expressed for my work yesterday continues to fuel my motivation. I am in awe of the profound changes my new writing approach has ignited, both on the page and within me.

With a smile, I enjoy a leisurely breakfast and a refreshing swim. I can already picture myself settled in the shady corner of the terrace, surrounded by the gentle hush of the Provence countryside, ready to dive into a day of writing.

The steam rises delicately as I refill my coffee, transforming the air around me into a fragrant embrace. The cool keys of my laptop beckon beneath my fingertips, and instantly, my narrative comes alive. Each word pulses with raw emotion, igniting the vivid colours of my imagination, intricately weaving together the essence of the journey I've created for my characters.

It's astonishing to consider that six months have slipped since I embarked on this project – six months spent wrestling with the anguish of James's betrayal and the oppressive weight of Barry's overbearing affection. Yet, against the odds, this chaotic struggle has metamorphosed into something profound, nourishing my very soul. The sense of accomplishment in this journey is truly inspiring.

Every keystroke isn't merely a way to heal; it's become my passion, my lifeline, and my characters are experiencing an exhilarating adventure that sweeps me off my feet. I can still hear the echoes of recognition from those I dared to share my work with yesterday – their enthusiastic whispers wrapped around my heart, stoking a fire within me. Their validation breathes life into my talent, undermining every moment of doubt I've faced. The transformative power of self-belief is truly empowering.

And these beautiful free butterflies – yes, they are all my own creations. Each one is meticulously crafted, bursting with the vibrancies of my experiences and dreams. They flutter about me, a vivid reminder that beauty and strength often emerge from the depths of pain.

'Wow, that was deep!' I whisper, lifting my cup to my lips, tilting it just enough to catch the last dregs of coffee lingering at the bottom. The warm liquid dances on my tongue, jolting me back to the present. I glance around, soaking in my surroundings, and can't help but marvel at the serendipity of it all. Who would have imagined I'd find myself on this incredible journey, thriving in the rich tapestry of the life I am courageously weaving, a life intertwined with the unyielding pursuit of my dreams?

Inspired by the French way of life and the ethereal beauty of the villa, my story unfolds. My characters spring to life, and as I close my eyes, they join me at the villa. All gather around the table, the clinking of glasses a merry symphony of cheers.

James, the engaging, charismatic and practised lover, effortlessly takes charge at the head of the table. His striking appearance and polished demeanour mask a far more sinister truth. Underneath the charm lies a darkness that hints at secrets and deception, making every interaction a delicate dance between allure and the chilling echoes of betrayal.

Next to him, shrouded in shadows at the 'dark end' of the table, sits Gavin – a man adrift in his own bitterness, awkwardness clinging to him like a second skin. Now, on his third marriage, he clutches to a woman half his age, desperately searching for a semblance of happiness that seems ever elusive.

And then there's Barry – on the surface, sweet, loyal, and unassuming, yet profoundly intense. I carry a weighty sense of guilt for not being able to love him as he truly deserves to be loved. His quiet devotion illuminated my path, but in my inability to reciprocate, I fear I dimmed something precious within him.

Across from my trio of lovers sit my vibrant new friends, Ruth, Carol, and Pierre. It's a thrilling first encounter for them with the men who have dramatically influenced my journey. They view Gavin as a pathetic, shallow man, while effortlessly undermining James's charm, challenging his grand declarations, and diminishing his bravado. I can see the irritation flicker across James's face; it's palpable, and I am loving it!

As for Barry, I can't quite figure out how they perceive him. Do they think I'm a fool for letting him slip away? Or do they see the intense, jealous control lurking beneath his facade of love and spontaneity, a man who speaks of adventures yet lives a far more predictable reality?

Amidst this tempest of emotions, I find comfort and strength in the presence of my family. My daughter casts suspicious glances at my lovers and completely ignores her father, creating tension, but they stand by me, a steadfast support system, endlessly loving and gloriously judgment-free. It's in this sanctuary that I can truly embrace who I am. Their unwavering love fuels me, transforming every challenge into a thrilling opportunity for triumph.

As the party unfolds, and after the initial tension, fuelled by the flavoursome French wine, this unlikely group weaves together and imagined chatter bursts forth like effervescent bubbles in a chilled glass of champagne. I choose to see this extraordinary scene as a vibrant testament to how far I have come; every soul here has played an integral role in my narrative, shaping the journey that has led me to this very moment.

It's late now, and the evening pulses with energy as I sip my wine, watching my imaginary guests whirl across the terrace like stars set alight. Carol twirls with James, laughter spilling from them like music. I smile, reassured in the knowledge that Carol is far too smart to fall for his charm! Pierre and Ruth glide in perfect sync as Gavin and Barry sit together, watching from the sidelines, an awkward silence vibrating like a taut string; they clearly do not like each other, and an unspoken tension is brewing beneath the surface.

The cicadas join in a symphony of sound that echoes through the olive trees, weaving a tapestry of memories and dreams. In this enchanted moment, I feel the thrill of connection and the bittersweet pang of nostalgia, knowing that these fleeting encounters are the very essence of our shared tapestry, vibrant and alive.

In this evening glow, the characters of my imagination seem the most tangible, their vivid personalities shining as brightly as the stars that begin to twinkle overhead. And I believe that this crazy, imaginary party will be etched in my heart forever.

Time has flown by, and my imaginary guests have visited me many times over the last ten days, but today is Friday, and the evening settles in like a thick fog, enveloping me in its stillness as I reflect on my final writing day. Crumpled notes, their edges worn and frayed, litter my workspace – evidence of countless hours wrestling with words. My fingers hover hesitantly above the keyboard, trembling with anticipation and dread. As I pen the last chapter, my imaginary guests, once vibrant and alive in my mind, begin to fade away, returning to their existence as mere characters on a page, leaving behind an echo of their stories that lingers in the air, bittersweet and haunting.

I lean back in my chair, rubbing my red-rimmed and weary eyes. The story that flowed so freely in my mind now feels stagnant, as if locked behind an impenetrable barrier of exhaustion, built from the countless hours of mental strain and the physical toll of late nights and early mornings. Whispers of doubt echo in the evening's stillness and taunt me with the fear that my work will never be good enough.

Glancing across the terrace, I watch the shadows stretch and yawn, inching across the patchwork of weathered stone. A sigh escapes my lips as I think of Ruth, her sharp eyes scanning my pages, seeking the brilliance I fear I haven't delivered well enough. The thought alone sends a shudder through me, tightening my chest.

'Was it worth the months of work and these late nights?' I mumble to myself, a grin tugging at my lips. The email to Ruth has been sent, and attached to it is my finished manuscript, which is also, in many ways, a reflection of my dreams for the future. The relief of completion washes over me, a tangible sense of accomplishment that I can't help but savour.

'So, of course it was!'

The world buzzes with possibilities, each shimmering in my mind like stars waiting to be wished upon. I smile as I envision all the adventures ahead. The anticipation of these future adventures fills me with excitement, a feeling I eagerly look forward to exploring. As I make my way to my bedroom, the familiar embrace of my cotton bedding beckons me. I sink into the softness, the weight of the day slipping away, and soon I drift into a deep slumber, wrapped in dreams that dance just beyond my reach.

Today is Saturday, and I have invited Ruth, Carol, and Pierre to the villa for lunch. The now-familiar warm breeze embraces me as I step out onto the sun-drenched terrace. The air is fragrant with the scent of blooming flowers and freshly cut herbs, mingling with the faint aroma of lunch wafting from the kitchen. I pluck a leaf from a nearby potted shrub, its coolness a pleasant contrast to the warmth of my skin. As I slowly close my eyes, the world around me fades. Only the sound of birds chirping and the whisper of the breeze remain. With a peaceful sigh, I breathe it all in, a contented smile creeping across my face. 'My little bit of paradise,' I murmur, savouring the moment of this sweet French embrace.

Ruth arrives first and strolls towards me, her eyes sparkling with enthusiasm. 'Congratulations, Jane. What a beautiful place this is, and lunch here is a perfect way to celebrate finishing your manuscript for your first novel.' She hands me a bottle of prosecco.

'Thank you, Ruth. But I don't think I'll need a grand celebration,' I say, taking a deep breath of the warm, floral air. Just feeling accomplished and standing here, enjoying and sharing this incredible place, is more than enough.

Carol and Pierre arrive, marching across the soft grass at the side of the Villa. I hear Carol giggle as Pierre attempts to open a bottle of wine, the cork popping free with a triumphant thud as they enter.

'See? That's the spirit!' Ruth nods towards them. 'You're all surrounded by love and laughter. And you've all earned this.'

With a grin, I sit at the table I've already set. My guests are real this time, and the table is set beautifully as sunlight dapples through the leaves of the ancient olive trees. 'You know, I'll miss this and you all when it's time to return home,' I admit, glancing around at the happiness enveloping us.

'Not a chance!' Carol chimes in with a glint in her eye. 'You'll have your completed manuscript, and we'll celebrate your book launch next. We'll do it all over again, but even bigger!'

'I can see it now,' I muse, feeling warmth in my chest. 'A crowd, a stage, all eyes on me...'

Pierre snorts softly, handing me a glass of the sparkling wine. 'But remember, you won't just be a dreamer then – you will be the author standing before them, sharing your story.'

I lift my glass, the sunlight catching the sparkling bubbles. 'To new beginnings,' I say, my voice steady but excitement bubbling beneath.

'To new beginnings!' they echo, and it feels like a promise wrapped in warmth – a moment savoured, a very special friendship celebrated.

The four of us laze around the terrace for the rest of the day, laughter spilling from our lips as the sun above us makes its way around the Villa.

Our creative spirits are alive and well, sparking laughter and inspiration. 'I can't believe you wrote a book about the characters in your village, Carol. Will you ever be able to go home?' Pierre chuckles, shaking his head. 'Can't wait to read more of your stuff!'

'Only if you promise us VIP tickets when your book becomes a play!' Carol shoots back with a playful grin.

We erupt into laughter that tugs at your heart, making time feel suspended. The music changes, a soft tune floating through the air, and without thinking, I stand up.

'Come on! Let's dance,' I call.

We spin and sway, losing ourselves in the rhythm as Charles Aznavour and 'She' booms out from my Alexa at Carol's request, our achievements worn proudly on our chests and inhibitions blurred by the alcohol.

LOVE, LIES AND BUTTERFLIES

Later, as we sit, slightly drunk and exhausted from dancing, the evening sky blankets the terrace in shades of deep blue, my guests gather their things, and the night air becomes heavy.

'I hate to say goodbye,' I admit, my heart sinking.

'Me too,' Carol replies, her voice soft but firm. 'These past few weeks have been magical.'

Ruth nods in agreement. 'Let's not let too much time pass before we do this again, okay?'

'Definitely,' I say, smiling through the bittersweet ache. 'We're special, all of us.' And as we step outside, towards the awaiting taxis, and embrace under the stars, there is an unspoken promise of more moments like this to come.

Chapter Twenty-Four – The Next Turning on the Road to Rediscovery

The sun is particularly harsh this morning as it pierces through the shutters. I squint against the brightness as I open them, and the gentle murmur of birds outside morphs into a deafening chorus. The rich aroma of my first freshly brewed coffee of the day, which I have placed on the ornate iron bedside table, fills the air, swirling around me and making me feel nauseous. The aftermath of my alcoholic indulgence yesterday weighs heavily on my head as I roll over in the cool cotton, fighting the urge to close my eyes and slip back into a heavy doze.

Yesterday was a whirlwind of laughter with my writing tribe, our chatter dancing like fireflies, but now, as I lay in this beautiful villa, a sense of emptiness has settled over me. My notebook sits silently beside me, its blank pages a reminder that the week ahead stretches like an uncharted sea – calm yet daunting, devoid of plans and purpose. The struggle of a writer trying to establish themselves in a world full of bestsellers and celebrities, and the fear of not knowing what the future holds, is all too real.

I trace the dust motes dancing in the air, lost in thought. As I revisit my story in my mind, its chapters are full of life and filled with characters that have mostly become my friends. For the past six months, stories of love, loss, and resilience have flourished within me, a vibrant extension of my thoughts and dreams. Now, they are taking on their own life while I stand still, an observer in their unfolding. In many ways, handing my story over to Ruth was like handing my children over to their teachers on the first day at school.

Pulling myself from the depths of my fog, I rise and stride purposefully toward the shimmering pool, its surface glistening like a promise. As I slip into the water's cool embrace, a rush of refreshment washes over me – a powerful reminder of the smart, vibrant woman I am striving to become. I embrace my swim; each stroke cuts through the surface with intent, the rhythmic motion of my arms banishing the remnants of my hangover.

Lengths blur together, and the world outside dissipates. Silence envelops me, broken only by my determination whispering through the stillness. Floating on my back, I surrender to the buoyancy as my body relaxes, and profound satisfaction swells within me, igniting a clarity of purpose. Each ripple is a bold testament to the distance I've travelled on this relentless journey of self-discovery.

As I leave the water and wander across the patio, the mug of now lukewarm coffee resting on the table beckons me. A pastry sits untouched, its flaky crust hinting at the sweet delight within. I settle at the table, feeling the warmth of the sunshine on my skin as I grab my notebook and flip it open, ready to map out my adventures for the week ahead.

I fire up Google and ponder the four sightseeing days stretching before me. I can already picture the vibrant streets and historic sites waiting to be explored.

My family will be arriving at the end of the week, their laughter and warmth set to fill the villa for a long weekend together. However, the clock continues to tick; I have just over a week left before I need to pack my things and journey back to Cherbourg, where the ferry awaits to take me home. I need to consider what my life will be like when I return to the UK. Still, for now, I am savouring this time and enjoying the tranquillity and peace of mind that it affords me as I pull out my pen and commit my sightseeing itinerary for the days ahead to the crisp pages of my trusty notebook before settling onto my sun lounger by the pool. No pressure, no deadlines – just pure bliss after a fantastic yet exhausting few weeks. Today is my Sunday off, and I fully commit to relaxation, savouring this time at the villa before heading to Avignon for dinner in the square.

The Camargue Tour

As I wake up on this Monday morning, excitement propels me out of bed. Today, I've booked a tour of the Camargue, and the thrill of the impending adventure fills me with joy.

The sun casts its warm embrace over the square's east side as I step into the vibrant throng, the anticipation crackling in the air. I join the queue for the bus marked with the promise of adventure, 'Camargue Tour' boldly etched on the windscreen.

'Can you believe this place?' A well-dressed man with a very handsome face, salt-and-pepper hair and a trim physique, who I would guess is likely around my age, stands in front of me in the queue and gestures with his arms wide towards the picturesque square as it awakens on this Monday morning.

'It's perfect,' I reply, grinning as he shakes my hand.

'By the way, it's Mark. I'm here on holiday and loving it; I'm not sure I'll want to go home next week.'

'Hi Mark, I'm Jane,' I reply instantly, noticing his bright smile as I tell him about my French adventure.

'Avignon is stunning! I've only just arrived here, but hear that the square lights up beautifully at dusk,' he says, a sparkle in his eye, as I reassure him that the sight before us comes alive in the evenings and is magical.

We are beckoned aboard by a driver who seems to have stepped straight out of a Parisian café, complete with a beret and stripey T-shirt; we settle into our seats, instinctively positioning ourselves together, and begin poring over the day's itinerary, our conversation flowing effortlessly between laughter and insight.

By the time we arrive in Arles, our first stop, it feels as if we have uncovered a hidden connection – we are both single, navigating the confusing waters of the dating scene from our respective corners of the UK. This French escape is more than a getaway; it is a journey of self-discovery, and with each moment spent together, we weave the threads of friendship amidst this vibrant Mediterranean backdrop.

'So, it's a walking tour in Arles first?' Mark points to the map on the back of the pamphlet that we are handed.

'Right, we have ninety minutes here, so shall we go and perhaps we can grab a coffee at some point? I can't wait to see where Van Gogh painted. Seeing the sights that inspired his work will be really interesting,' I say, my excitement growing. Mark smiles, falling into step next to me as if it's the most natural thing to do.

Arles doesn't disappoint, nor does Mark's company; we chat, laugh and share the wonder of this beautiful city before gratefully returning to the air conditioning in the bus, eager for the next stop, the Camargue National Park.

The bus rumbles through the countryside, the air thick with the earthy scent of orange dust. Outside, the vibrant landscapes unfold like a painter's canvas, splashes of bright pink flamingos dotting the salt flats. 'Wow! Can you believe the sheer number of flamingos in that one spot?' Mark exclaims, leaning eagerly across me, his enthusiasm infectious.

'I'm just as excited about the black bulls and white horses!' I reply, my heart racing as cherished childhood memories rise to the surface. 'Remember that TV show set here? The theme tune still gives me chills!' A wave of nostalgia washes over me, painting my thoughts with laughter from simpler times.

We gaze in awe at the majestic white horses as they canter in herds across the barren landscape and the prize-fighter physiques of the imposing bulls standing sedately, watching us watching them. As the minibus meanders through the national park, it feels as though we're slipping through a time portal, culminating with us disembarking the bus and crossing the drawbridge into the walled city of Aigues Mortes. With every step forward, we're pulled deeper into history, sheltered by the formidable ramparts that stand guard over centuries of stories, ready to unveil their secrets.

'It's great that we have enough time for a long lunch here. History, food, great company and a view?' Mark laughs. 'What more could we want?'

I smile in reply, and we embark on an adventure through the narrow alleys, browsing the charming shops and bars nestled within the walls. A tour of the ramparts guides us to a quaint square, where another delightful French bistro beckons us to bask in the sunshine and savour their exquisite fare.

What a magical day it has been! With a smile, I reflect on our return to Avignon with Mark, our hearts full of stories. We've experienced the wonders of wildlife in the national park, marvelled at the towers and ramparts, enjoyed the film set charm of Aigues-Mortes, and embraced the tranquillity of a beach stroll at Saintes-Maries-de-la-Mer.

We have taken so many photos, and as we sit in a bar in Avignon, time flies as we share them. This inevitably means sharing WhatsApp details, leading to plans to meet again tomorrow for our next adventure: a day exploring Marseille, which is about a ninety-minute drive away.

'I have had a wonderful day today,' Mark says earnestly as we part, his eyes sparkling with a warmth that makes my heart flutter. Overcome by a sudden wave of emotion, I hug him tightly and plant a soft kiss on his cheek, feeling a rush of connection between us.

'It truly has been lovely,' I reply, my voice almost a whisper, and I find myself promising him that tomorrow will be just as amazing, if not more so.

As I turn away, a flurry of butterflies dances wildly in my stomach and my mind races with thoughts of all the possibilities. Each step toward my car feels heavy with anticipation and uncertainty. I remind myself to learn from the lessons of the past and tread carefully, thinking with my head rather than my heart. I need to take my time to truly understand this intoxicating man who has captivated me so swiftly, and resolve not to revert to type, and allow my overly romantic imagination to create a future with him, no matter how tempting it may be. I shall instead embrace it for what it is, the fleeting magic of one unforgettable day.

Back at the villa, I sink into my lounger with a cold glass of wine, basking in the evening sun. Reflecting on the day's events, a sense of contentment washes over me. Today was unplanned, unexpected, exciting, and pure bliss!

Marseille

As I sift through my wardrobe, my alarm buzzes, and I glance at the time – 8:45 AM. 'No way I'm going to be late or not looking my best for my second date with Mark,' I mumble, heart racing, as I decide on a pretty fitted sundress and slip it on.

Outside, the gravel crunches beneath my strappy wedges, the sound echoing in the quiet morning. I turn just in time to see a sleek silver Porsche glide to a stop, the sunlight bouncing off its polished surface. My stomach flips as Mark steps out, his cologne mingling with the morning air. He looks confident and sun-kissed.

'Hey there,' he says with a grin, striding toward me.

'Hi!' I beam back, as he envelops me in a brief embrace and plants a soft kiss on my cheek. It leaves me giddy yet slightly flustered.

'Ready for our adventure part two?' His eyes sparkle with mischief as he takes my hand, fingers intertwining, and we head to the car.

"Ready as I'll ever be!" I giggle nervously, my tongue flicking out to moisten my lips. As we settle into the luxurious leather seats, the intoxicating aroma of 'new' car wraps around me like a warm embrace. In that moment, all the cautionary lessons that my association with James should have instilled in me—warnings about the pitfalls of wealth and the illusions it can create—are suddenly whisked away onto the floral summer breeze.

Mark turns the key, and the powerful electric engine hums to life. 'Listen to that, silence.... Just picked this beauty up before the trip down here,' he says, a mischievous grin spreading across his face. 'Want to hear the Formula One version?' He presses a button, and the engine noise roars. 'Ultimate midlife crisis car!' he adds with a chuckle.

'Well, I'm sure I'll enjoy sharing your midlife crisis today!' I laugh excitedly. As we devour the miles toward Marseille, I barely notice the views rushing by.

'So, what's first on our agenda?' I ask, my gaze fixed on his toned, tanned arms and legs.

'The Old Port,' he replies, eyes twinkling. 'But I've got a few hidden gems in mind, too, so I hope that you are up for some exploring?'

'Absolutely! I've heard the Mucem is impressive, and I'm looking forward to seeing Notre Dame de la Garde!'

'Perfect! We'll make a day of it,' he says, a playful smirk dancing on his lips. 'Get ready; I've done my homework on the authentic Marseille.'

With each mile we travel towards Marseille, the thrill of adventure envelops me, and I can't help but feel fortunate to get the chance to share this day with him.

As we approach the city, the sights begin to unfold around us. 'Marseille's got so much history,' he remarks, glancing out the window. 'You'll love the Old Port, but trust me, the real treasures are off the beaten path.'

'Like what?' I lean closer, intrigued.

'I'll show you. The architecture of the Vallon des Auffes and La Major Cathedral is breathtaking,' he replies, confidently spinning the steering wheel with one hand as he manoeuvres our steed into the tiniest parking space.

'I'm all in! Let's discover it all!' I say, grinning from ear to ear as we glide into the heart of Marseille, ready for the adventure that awaits.

Marseille is a city rich in history and culture, a vibrant tapestry of local life and international influence. All of yesterday's reservations about being guarded and protecting my heart from disappointment disappear as my hand slips comfortably into Mark's and we explore the colourful and chaotic Old Port. It's bursting with locals trying to make a living and tourists seeking to capture some quintessential French charm. Still, despite the chaos, a friendly cafe welcomes us for our first harbourside coffee of the day. I love being here with Mark; he embraces everything around us with passion and excitement, and I find myself hanging on to his every word.

The next stop is La Major Cathedral, with its Moorish architecture and symbolism, before heading back to the water for lunch at Vallon des Auffes, a hidden cove featuring rows of small, brightly painted fishing boats, sculptures, and authentic restaurants. The aroma of freshly caught seafood and Mediterranean spices fills the air, enticing our taste buds. We settle in at a quaint restaurant, the sound of the sea trickling onto the nearby rocky beach providing a refreshing backdrop to our easy conversation over the meal.

Our tour concludes with a march in the afternoon sun up to the Mucem, Notre-Dame de la Garde, on the hill above the city. There, we take in the history and French charm on display, then admire the amazing late-afternoon views of the city beneath us.

As we head for home, the Porsche propels forward, its engine quiet and melodic. Our chatter fills the cockpit, blending with the soft rustle of the air as the car in Mark's very capable hands effortlessly cuts its way through the sea breeze and navigates the winding coastal roads.

Mark

As we approach Jolie Retraite, the gravel driveway crunches beneath the tyres, sounding like gentle applause welcoming us home. I catch myself smiling, unwilling to let go of this moment – the thought of the day ending tugs at my heart, and an idea bubbles inside me. And so, with a casual flick of my wrist, I gesture toward the inviting pool.

"Care for a drink? Maybe we can take a dip?" I propose, my voice bubbling with excitement. It feels so effortless to invite him in; after all, it's just two friends enjoying the afternoon, and stretching out the warmth of the day sounds perfect.

Taking a steadying breath, I remind myself that I'm a confident woman in control. My heart flutters with a hint of anticipation as I steal a glance at Mark, a playful smile playing at the corners of my lips. "The bathroom's right over there if you want to change," I say, gesturing toward it, my tone light yet assertive.

The air in my bedroom is filled with the soft scent of sunscreen and the faint hint of my favourite coconut lotion. I pull out my go-to swimming costume – a vibrant splash of colour that always brings out my confidence. Sliding into it feels like hidden armour, empowering me as I catch my reflection and strike a quick pose; my French suntan looks good on me.

The sun gleams off Mark's tanned skin when he reappears, and I'm not going to lie: it has quickened my pulse. A mischievous grin spreads across my face as I take his hand firmly. Together, we walk to the pool's edge, the sound of water lapping against the sides pulls at our excitement. With a shared glance that speaks volumes, we leap into the crisp, refreshing water, splashing and laughing as we break the surface.

The sun glints off the water as Mark launches himself forward with a jubilant splash.

His laughter echoes around the terrace.

I chuckle, feeling the coolness enliven me as he swims closer. 'You're like a kid again!'

He grins, his eyes sparkling. 'What can I say? The water brings out the child in me!'

LOVE, LIES AND BUTTERFLIES

Suddenly, he reaches out, pulling me into the splash, droplets flying everywhere. 'Hey!' I laugh, trying to catch my breath.

'Come on, don't be shy!' He tugs me closer, his fingers brushing against my arms, igniting an ember that has been quietly glowing within me.

'Okay, okay, I'm coming!' I lean in, and he wraps his arms around me, pulling me into a warm embrace that sends me into a spin.

'I could do this all day,' he murmurs, his breath warm against my neck.

'Me too,' I reply softly.

He tilts his head, our lips graze.... 'Let's take this somewhere more comfortable.'

I nod as he leads me to the sun lounger. The sun bathes us in its warmth as we kiss passionately, which inevitably leads to him pulling my swimming costume to the floor and expertly exploring my body. I tug at his swim shorts, and electricity buzzes between us. My hands explore him in return; the world stops, and in that moment, all that matters is our raw, passionate, and urgent lovemaking.

Sated, happy and just ever so slightly overwhelmed, I nestle against him, my fingertips gliding over the contours of his firm chest. Spent and very hot from our lovemaking, we're perched precariously on the narrow sunbed, and a soft chuckle escapes my lips. 'Guess we're a little past our prime for sunbed escapades,' I tease. 'But let's be honest, we wouldn't have made it to the bedroom!' My breathless laughter dances in the air.

Mark leans closer, his breath warm against my skin as he whispers, 'You know, I didn't plan this.' His blue eyes sparkle with a mix of mischief and sincerity. I feel my heart race, the space between us still charged with electric tension.

He brushes a stray hair behind my ear, his fingers lingering just a touch longer than necessary. 'But,' he continues, a teasing smile tugging at his lips, 'I just couldn't help myself.' His gaze holds mine, filled with an intensity that makes it hard to look away.

'Are you sure you didn't?' I challenge playfully, arching an eyebrow.

Mark chuckles, leaning in even closer, 'What can I say? Sometimes, desire takes over, and self-control disappears.'

The sun glints on the water as he untangles himself from our perched position, muscles rippling beneath his skin. With a playful grin, he grabs my hand and pulls me to my feet. 'Come on, I am very hot!!' he says with a laugh, manoeuvring me back into the pool.

'Oh yes, you definitely are very hot!' I reply with a giggle.

As we splash down, the cool water envelops us, and I find myself wrapping my arms and my naked body around him. 'This feels amazing,' I whisper.

'Yes? It's paradise,' he replies, his voice soothing against the gentle sounds of the water.

Just the two of us, floating together, lost in each other. I close my eyes and sink deeper into his embrace. 'I am feeling so alive right now,' I admit, a smile creeping onto my lips.

He holds me a little tighter, a satisfied grin playing at the corners of his mouth. 'Good. That's exactly how it's supposed to be.'

LOVE, LIES AND BUTTERFLIES

The afternoon gives way to evening as Mark leans against the kitchen counter, a towel casually slung around his waist. 'So, what's in that antique-looking fridge of yours?'

I open the door, the cool air wafting over us, and pull out a few leftover dishes. 'Nothing fancy, but I have some cheese and pasta from last night.'

His eyes twinkle as he reaches for a bottle of wine sitting on the counter. 'Perfect! I'll handle the wine if you take care of the food.'

'Deal.' I laugh, watching as he pours us each a glass of the rich crimson liquid.

Later, we settle on the couch, nibbling on cheese and sipping wine. 'You know,' he says, leaning closer, 'this feels surprisingly comfortable and very nice.'

I smirk, brushing my fingers against his. 'You mean the company or the food?'

'Both,' he replies, his voice dropping to a softer tone. 'But I think the company is winning.'

A blush creeps up my cheeks as I smile. 'Well, I'm glad you like it.'

As the evening unfolds, we share kisses and gentle embraces, and I feel a warmth blooming between us that feels both comfortable and exhilarating. Our towels slip away, forgotten as the tide of passion rises again. Mark reaches for my hand, our fingers intertwining, and he asks softly, 'Do you want to show me your bedroom?'

My heart races at the invitation, a thrill coursing through me. 'I thought you'd never ask,' I reply, my voice barely above a whisper, laced with excitement and a hint of vulnerability.

We tumble into the room, laughter bubbling up and spilling over like champagne, contrasting sharply with the serene stillness that envelops us. Our bodies naturally intertwine when we finally sink into the crisp white linens, and the outside world dissolves into a blur. Mark's eyes, warm and inviting, reflect a joy that surges within me.

'This was a great idea,' he murmurs, his voice soft yet clear, locking onto mine with an intensity that sends shivers down my spine.

'Agreed,' I reply, a smile playing on my lips as a rush of tenderness wraps around us like a delicate silk sheet. It's more than mere attraction; it feels like a dance of souls, gracefully weaving together.

The night stretches before us, filled with the thrill of whispered passion and soft caresses. I can hear the rapid rhythm of our hearts, a quiet melody that blends into a symphony of intimacy. Every embrace holds a promise, and our glances are filled with unspoken emotions. I feel truly moved by the beauty of this moment we're creating together. In a moment of weakness, I find myself eagerly anticipating many more meaningful moments like this with this wonderful man. But isn't that how it has all gone so wrong before?

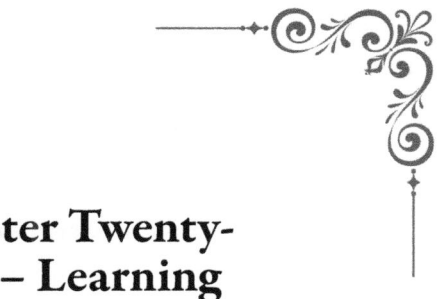

Chapter Twenty-Five – Learning From the Past

It's early the following day, and I sit in bed, sheets tangled around my legs, as I watch Mark place two mugs of coffee on the bedside tables and fling open the shutters. His unabashed nakedness is only matched by the playful smirk on his face.

'You're definitely going to smile like that after what we just did!' I tease, trying to keep my tone light.

He chuckles, running a hand through his hair. 'Why not? That was incredible. You were incredible, we were incredible!'

I roll my eyes, but my lips betray me, curling into a smile. 'I should probably be upset with myself, you know. Just giving in like that.'

He raises an eyebrow, stepping closer. 'Giving in? Or perhaps embracing your sexuality?'

I bite my lip, leaning back against the headboard. 'It feels a little reckless. I barely know you.'

'True,' he concedes, his expression softening. 'But don't you think that makes it all the more exciting?'

As Mark leans across to hand me a cup of coffee, his fingers brush mine, and that familiar flutter starts in my stomach. The same flutter I'd felt with James and Barry. Warning signals flash across my mind.

'This is lovely,' I say, pulling my hand back slightly.

'It is,' he agreed, his eyes warm with interest.

I take a deep breath. 'I should probably tell you... I'm just getting my life back together after some complicated relationships.' The words feel strange in my mouth – I usually dismiss the lessons of the past and fall madly in love at this point in a relationship.

Mark's smile widens. 'That makes two of us. My divorce isn't even final.'

I nod, surprised at my sense of relief. This could be a holiday connection – no pressure, no expectations. Finally, I do not need to project a future onto every man I meet. Maybe that is what growth looks like – enjoying the moment without needing it to be forever.

After a cosy breakfast, Mark leaves. His road trip is taking him onto the west coast of France tomorrow, and the Porsche slides down the drive, its tyres crackling on the gravel. We had such a great time together; we clicked in a way that surprised me. And I don't know if I will ever see him again. This new me, this new confidence in relationships, is liberating. It's taken a while, but I have finally learned from my past mistakes and now found confidence in my sexuality.

I picture Mark often throughout the day. Perhaps he is thinking about me and smiling, too. I am sure he is, but it also doesn't matter if he is enjoying his trip, and I have completely slipped his mind.

The lingering scent of intimacy hangs in the air inside the villa today, and the crumpled sheets lie scattered like my thoughts. 'Time to tackle the beds first,' I declare as I bundle away the sheets from last night and smooth freshly laundered spare bedding across the memories of the night before with purpose.

As the day progresses, I consciously set aside thoughts of Mark, redirecting my energy to the joyful reunion that awaits me tomorrow with my family. 'I can't wait to see their faces; I've missed them so much,' I whisper, a genuine smile spreading. My heart is filled with joy as I envision wrapping my arms around my children and grandchildren and immersing myself in the pure, unconditional love that family brings.

Grabbing my keys, I drive to the supermarket with purpose. 'Let's stock up,' I declare, a wave of determination surging through my veins. As I push open the shop's glass doors, a warm, intoxicating blend of fresh bread and baked goods wafts towards me, beckoning me toward the bread counter. 'This is it; I'm going to spoil them all!' I exclaim, taking hold of my trolley, a sturdy red and black companion for my shopping adventure, and fill it with an array of delectable treats and colourful delights, each item chosen for the joy it will bring to those I love.

With the villa cleaned and supplies neatly arranged, I finally find a moment to swim. I am still smiling and embracing my identity as a strong, independent woman who has just had a very liberating encounter with an incredibly charming and attractive man. But soon, I will return to the familiar roles of mum and nanny for four whole glorious days.

After my swim, I sit by the pool's edge, the sun glinting off the water. I try to relax, but flashbacks of the previous evening keep visiting my mind. Mark's laughter echoes, invigorating me, while memories of the warmth of his body remind me of my passionate surrender. The thrill of our uncomplicated intimacy is intoxicating,

The old me would have sent Mark numerous text messages by now. I am still a work in progress, but I manage to keep myself busy and resist that urge. What we had was wonderful, intoxicating, and liberating, but it's over, and I shall treasure it as a memory; let him go and move on.

Chapter Twenty-Six
– Family Time

Laughter spills from the driveway. 'Mum! We're here!' Sarah's high and excited voice carries through the air.

I step outside, my heart light. 'Come in; I can't wait to see you all!' I call out with a smile.

The minivan door swings open, and my grandchildren tumble out. 'Look! I got a new swim float!' Lily shouts, waving it overhead like a trophy.

'Well, I've got croissants!' I announce playfully, holding a plate of warm, flaky pastry aloft, enticing their taste buds.

'Croissants? Yummy!' Josh yells as the kids dart toward me, arms outstretched.

'Careful, you'll knock me over!' I laugh as they barrel into one of my favourite hugs, but they're too excited to listen. 'Watch the coffee!' I shout, chuckling as they skim past the table, narrowly avoiding the steaming coffee pot I've just prepared.

But within seconds of arrival, my beautiful grandchildren are splashing into the pool. 'Look at me bomb, Nanny!' Josh hollers, sending water flying everywhere.

'Hey! You're getting my croissants wet!' I laugh, shaking my head. 'Alright, you little fish, just don't drown before brunch!' I call over the splashes, revelling in their joy.

Mark drifts into my mind momentarily, but I brush him away purposefully as I look at my now-adult children, Sarah and Matt, and their partners, Joe and Emily, gathered around the table. 'Who wants a croissant?' I offer, holding the golden pastry like a prize.

My daughter Sarah urges, 'Mum, tell us everything about your French adventure. Are you hiding some French Prince Charming in a cupboard somewhere?' I see the eager curiosity in their eyes.

'I wish!' I retort, avoiding her eye contact. 'You'll be sick of hearing about my time here by the end of the weekend!' I reply, smiling. So much has happened that I am unsure where to begin.

As we settle, chatting and soaking up the sun, I watch my grandchildren enjoying the pool. 'You're going to exhaust yourselves!' I say, shaking my head in mock disapproval.

'Never! This is the best day ever!' Lily laughs, and I can't help but smile.

In this moment, surrounded by my family, I realise that times like this – filled with laughter, sunshine, and love – are all I need. My heart swells. I wouldn't trade this chaos for anything.

The day is full of fun. My happy brood loves the villa as much as I do, and I easily slip back into mum and nanny mode and love every minute of it.

As evening approaches, the terrace takes on a magical glow, and this time my guests are real, not imaginary. The air is filled with the clinking of plates and the gentle rustling of leaves in the light evening breeze. Matt, my boy (he may be thirty now, but he will always be my boy), leans back in his chair, a smile lighting up his face. 'Remember that time we stayed at the 'French Life' campsite near here, and you fell out of the boat when we went canoeing, Sarah?' he says with a chuckle, shaking his head.

Sarah rolls her eyes playfully. 'That must have been about twenty years ago, and you mean when you insisted we take that 'shortcut' and ended up trying to row against a current that tipped me out of the boat?' Her infectious laughter pulls me back to a scene that happened long ago.

'Hey, I was trying to be adventurous!' Matt defends himself, throwing up his hands in mock surrender. I can't help but smile, the warmth of the memories wrapping around my bare shoulders like a light summer pashmina.

'Adventurous or trying to drown your sister?' I tease, and the table erupts into more laughter. 'We discovered that fabulous little café, remember? With the best langoustine ever, followed by gelato?' I remind them.

'Right!' Sarah exclaims, her eyes sparkling. 'That gelato was a game changer. We should do that again sometime.'

'Definitely,' I say, my heart full of belonging. My voice softens as I add, 'You know, I wouldn't trade these moments for anything. It's funny how life takes us on these wild rides, but it's the people we love and make memories with that ground us and make us special.'

'We've come a long way as a family,' Sarah replies, glancing at everyone around the table.

Matt raises his glass, a mischievous glint in his eye. 'To wild rides and unforgettable memories!'

'To us!' the others chime in, and we clink our glasses together, the sound a joyful promise. At this moment, under the olive tree, we are not just okay; we are thriving, fulfilled, and happy, celebrating the beauty of life and the power of being together.

As the now-familiar sun clock moves around the villa, the adult laughter dances through the air; the kids chase fireflies, their giggles breaking the evening stillness in the most perfect way possible.

And as darkness settles and wine flows, I can feel myself relaxing. I am exhausted, but I don't want this day to end. It appears that this sentiment is shared by us all; even the children are now running on pure adrenaline, determined not to fall asleep in case they miss something.

The long weekend unfolds like a vibrant tapestry woven with laughter, delectable food, and cherished moments. We relish exploring both beloved haunts from holidays past and discovering new gems that spark our curiosity. Yet, amidst the joy, this beautiful time together slips away like sand through a sieve, fleeting and ephemeral. As twilight descends upon our final evening at 'Jolie Retraite', a bittersweet pang tugs at my heart, reminding me how quickly these precious moments can fade into memory.

'Are we going home tomorrow, Nanny?' Josh asks, his eyes glistening with unshed tears. It breaks my heart to see that genuine sadness reflected on his face.

LOVE, LIES AND BUTTERFLIES 213

I nod slowly, my own heart heavy with the weight of this impending goodbye. 'Yes, you are, buddy. But we have had so much fun, haven't we?'

'Best holiday ever!' Lily beams, her bright smile lighting up the room. Despite the looming farewell, I can't help but smile back at my quirky-spirited granddaughter. Her laughter feels like sunshine, a tender reminder of how much I love them both.

I soak in these final, precious moments, and before I know it, Monday morning arrives, and I find myself standing by the door, watching my family gather their things like precious treasures, each item a reminder of the memories we've forged.

'Do you have everything?' I ask, my voice trembling as I try to stay composed amidst the storm of emotions swirling within me.

'I think so!' Josh chirps, tossing his backpack over his shoulder with youthful eagerness, but then he pauses – his face clouded with worry. 'Wait – where's my favourite dinosaur?'

I smile softly, already knowing the answer. 'Um, check under your bed,' I suggest gently.

'I'll be home soon!' I call out, my heart aching as I offer hugs that feel like lifelines as they peel away.

'Mum! We'll FaceTime you tomorrow before you leave for your drive back to Cherbourg on Wednesday!' Sarah promises, her grin from the back seat a flicker of comfort in the bittersweet moment.

As their minivan disappears down the lane, I return to the profound stillness of the villa, a sharp contrast to the vibrant, noisy, and messy past few days. Biting my lip, I remind myself that I'll be following them home later this week, and much as

I hate to leave Provence, this weekend has reminded me that I am ready to call an end to this particular adventure and go home to my family.

Chapter Twenty-Seven – The Adventure is the Journey, Not the Destination

It's my last full day in Provence. I busy myself around the villa, tidying away remnants of my stay. Today is all about packing and cleaning. 'Focus,' I whisper to myself, momentarily missing Gavin's regimental check-and-double-check mentality as I eye the half-full suitcase in the corner of the room.

I stroll to the fridge, pulling the door open and chuckling. 'No clearing out needed here!' One lonely piece of cheese sits in the centre, saving itself for a grand finale. 'Classic move,' I murmur, remembering my son's knack for emptying a fridge back home. It's obviously a child's prerogative, no matter how old they are.

As I tidy up, I let Vernon Kay's familiar voice fill the air. I have missed his show over the last month, and tuning in again on my laptop feels like a first step in my homeward journey. His light banter accompanies me while I sort through what to pack and what to clean or put in the rubbish.

'Not much longer now,' I remind myself, heart fluttering with anticipation – and a hint of nerves – until my farewell dinner with Ruth in Avignon tonight. 'She's promised to give me some early feedback on my manuscript. Just breathe; you can do this.' The thought of the evening with Ruth, the feedback on my manuscript, and the impending departure tomorrow fills me with excitement and nerves.

'What a time this has been,' I say, pausing to take in the sun-baked view from my window. The memories of this place, the people I've met, and the experiences I've had flood my mind. 'But all adventures have to come to an end, and tomorrow morning, the end of mine will be as I hit the road and drive back to Cherbourg in time for my Thursday evening ferry home.' I nod to myself. 'Let's ensure this ending is just as memorable as the rest of my French adventure.'

I finish packing my bags late afternoon and line them up neatly in the hallway. The sun, which has been my constant companion in my time here, filters through the half-open shutters and glows on the villa's bare floor. I glance at my watch – just enough time for one last swim before I head into Avignon to meet Ruth.

As I arrive at the pretty café, I spot Ruth seated at one of the pavement tables. She is chatting animatedly with the waitress in fluent French, her arms flailing, and her laughter mingling with the clinking of glasses. The scene is cosy, and Ruth is glowing. I hurry over, and we embrace tightly.

'The master and her apprentice!' I say with a grin, sliding into the chair across from her.

Ruth beams and, with a flourish, pushes a glass of cold white wine toward me. 'One I made earlier!' She winks, her eyes sparkling with mischief.

I lift the glass, savouring the crisp aroma. 'You are a friend in a million!'

We order our meals, and Ruth leans in, her voice animated. 'I just can't get over your characters. They pulled me in! The way their stories intertwine is very clever and really quite addictive!' Her hands gesture familiarly as she speaks. 'You are very talented, Jane,' she reassures me. 'Reading your story is like I'm on an adventure with you, feeling every thrill. But I think you could expand on a few details here and there,' she suggests, her tone becoming softer, almost conspiratorial.

I nod eagerly, excitement bubbling within me. 'What do you think I should add?'

She shares her ideas, and I can feel my confidence swelling with each suggestion. 'Wow, I never thought of it that way,' I say, my voice barely above a whisper, filled with awe.

Ruth leans back, a satisfied smile on her lips. 'It's really good, Jane, and I'd love to be your mentor and help you polish this, make it shine and get it out into the world.'

'Really? Thank you so much; that will be amazing.' I can hardly contain my excitement.

'Of course! You are my pupil, so your success will shine on me!' She clinks her glass against mine. 'Let's cement this partnership over a delicious dinner and soak in all this "Frenchness" around us.'

As we toast, the excitement for our future project overflows. I can already envision the books we will write together. We share a lovely evening. Ruth will be following me back to the UK at some point soon, meaning that we part ways with a fond farewell for now rather than a goodbye.

I lay in the iron bed that dominates the bedroom at the villa for the final time. Ruth's words echo in my mind, igniting a wildfire of excitement within me. Sleep eludes me; instead, I'm consumed by a whirlwind of possibilities – each one more vibrant than the last, flickering like a kaleidoscope behind my closed eyelids.

When dawn peeks through the shutters and the birds serenade me with their final French chorus, I leap from the bed, fuelled by a surge of unexplainable energy, considering I have hardly slept. Moving swiftly, almost instinctively, I pack my car with bags that seem to hold more than just belongings. Each item slides into place flawlessly, as if it has enjoyed my adventure as much as I have but is now ready to go home.

As I step outside, the cool morning air embraces me one last time, just like an old friend, invigorating my spirit. I take one last look at the villa, its charm etched in my memory, and slip the key beneath the mat with a deep, bittersweet sigh. It feels heavy, laden with the weight of memories, and as I turn away, my heart races with exhilaration. A new adventure awaits, and I can't help but feel that this is just the beginning.

As I embark on my journey, my satnav's cheerful voice directs me toward the motorway, and a vast 700-kilometre extravaganza of the French countryside unfolds. The landscape transforms before my eyes – fields of vibrant blue lavender give way to golden blooms, and soon, lush vineyards stretch endlessly, rolling past my window like masterful strokes on an artist's canvas. This day is not just another mark on the calendar; it represents a powerful new beginning – my return home – and I feel complete, accomplished, and at peace with myself.

At 5 pm, I step into the boutique hotel in Poitiers, where the air is infused with the soothing scents of fresh linens and blooming flowers from the courtyard. Soft, ambient music washes over me, and a long, cool shower revives my weary body after a seven-hour drive.

Outside the hotel, the cobblestone streets pulse with the whispers of the city's rich history, yet the evening shadows arrive far too soon. Choosing simplicity, I indulge in a warm baguette, its crust crackling against my teeth as I savour each bite on a bench overlooking a picturesque park. The moment is sweet and serene, yet exhaustion calls me back to my cosy room, where the plush bed awaits. Sinking into the soft pillows, I feel the world slip away, the remnants of the delicious bread lingering on my palate as I drift into a profound, peaceful slumber.

It is later than I had intended when the morning sun's dancing glow teases me awake. The distant clang of a church bell punctuates the air, framing the melodic laughter of children that echoes through the cobbled streets. Outside, café patrons share whispers over steaming cups, their voices blending into the morning symphony. The delicious scent of pastries wafts in, coaxing me from the comfort of my sheets, and the complimentary breakfast does not disappoint before the road beckons – 500 more kilometres to Cherbourg, where I will meet a ferry that will carry me home.

The final French leg of my journey is slick and uneventful, and it is not until I drive onto the ferry that the rain starts to fall softly, the cool droplets washing dust and flies from my windscreen. The rain and the cool sea breeze are refreshing after so many hot, dry days.

And we are off – seven long hours until Portsmouth. I glance around the deck, absorbing the view of Cherbourg and France for one last time, and feel a tinge of sadness as it slips away.

I mentally navigate my priorities. Since I haven't booked a cabin, and it's an overnight crossing, finding a seat in the lounge is crucial, so I scan the area, aware of the throngs of other passengers also searching for comfort.

Just sixty minutes into the journey, as France fades into a hazy outline and I awkwardly spill coffee down my white T-shirt, I hear a voice breaking through my thoughts: 'Fancy bumping into you!'

I spin around to see Mark sliding into the recently vacated seat beside me. A rush of heat floods my cheeks, and my mind races as I fumble for words.

But before I can gather my thoughts, Mark continues, into what sounds like a pre-rehearsed speech, his voice steady yet tinged with vulnerability: 'I enjoyed our time together. I feel a genuine connection with you and believe we could be truly special together. It's just that neither of us is in the right place to embark on another relationship. For both of us, it's just too soon.'

His honesty resonates deeply within me. After what feels like an eternity of reflection, I find the words to respond. 'I felt something real for you too, but I have been so hurt in the past and made so many mistakes in relationships that I am just trying to be grown up, and a bit more guarded from now on.'

Mark takes my hand. Warmth spreads through me, and I don't pull away. His smile is disarming, and I can't help but return it. 'We are both a bit out of practice in dating etiquette,' he jokes softly, but I can sense the sincerity behind his words.

We navigate the journey back to Blighty together. As the ferry glides across the English Channel, laughter dances between us, intertwining with the stories we share about our hopes, our dreams, and the lives we're returning to. Each word deepens our connection, and by the end of the journey, we commit to being friends, bound by a mature and beautiful French liaison.

Chapter Twenty-Eight - Pieces of a Puzzle

Stepping through the door of my little house, I'm welcomed by the familiar scent of home, momentarily relieving the weariness of a sleepless night on the boat. The hastily made mug of coffee, a comforting weight in my hands, further brings a sense of homecoming.

But before long, my body yearns for the sanctuary of my bed. That soft haven where the world fades away beckons to me, promising solace after a month's absence. I feel the sheets enveloping me, pulling me into a deep sleep where my vivid and tangled dreams replay the fragments of the last decade – the moments that shaped me.

It all begins with Gavin. His betrayal hangs like a cloud, his inability to stand firm shoving me toward the edge. I can see his face, the shadow of his indecision etched into my mind. That weakness, once so painful, becomes the spark igniting my fight for myself and my family.

The next piece of my puzzle is James. His eyes cold as ice, betraying nothing but a glimmer of mischief, a calculating and manipulative mind behind the charming smile. I feel the weight of his gaze, an invisible string pulling me closer, and I close my eyes to the sharp edges hidden beneath his polished exterior.

Our conversations twist like smoke, enchanting yet suffocating. They are like smoke in the sense that they were elusive, constantly changing shape and form, making it difficult for me to grasp the truth. Each word is laced with a subtle sting that I foolishly mistake for wisdom. I lean in, eager to unravel the mystery of him, unaware that I am merely a pawn in his game. The lessons come wrapped in a seductive charm, each one a bitter pill that cracks my innocence wide open.

With each ultimate revelation, I feel parts of myself shift, a painful metamorphosis unfurling in the shadow of his influence. These revelations are not grand epiphanies but subtle realisations that chip away at my innocence. My laughter fades, replaced by a steely resolve I never knew I possessed. The scars he left are not just reminders of my naivety; they are badges of survival, evidence of a story that twisted and turned in ways I'd never imagined possible.

James led me to Barry, the private investigator. He starkly contrasts the fraudster I'm trying to track down. Barry exudes kindness, loyalty, and a quiet availability that draws me in. He's always there, ready to listen, ready to help. But our relationship is more than just professional. There's a bond, a connection that goes beyond the case we're working on.

Yet, as I bask in his safety, a feeling grips my chest – a slow suffocation. His protective nature, while initially comforting, becomes a weight. I find myself wanting to breathe, to escape the cocoon he wraps around me. I look into his eyes and see unspoken hope. It pierces my heart, and I know I can't stay. In an instant, the words tumble out, jagged and sharp. I watch his expression shatter, the hurt spilling over as I struggle to justify my decision to break his heart.

Breaking up with Barry hits me hard, and I grab a pen and pour my emotions onto paper. Each stroke of my pen ultimately transported me to France, to Provence's sun-drenched, picturesque landscape. The vibrance of Avignon and the 'Jolie Retraite' beckon me as I step inside, ready to embrace this new chapter filled with inspiration and beauty.

The air is filled with the rich aroma of garlic and herbs, and each meal feels like a celebration– fresh tomatoes, silky olive oil, and exquisite wine that dances on my palate. At Château Anaïs, I immerse myself in a writing course surrounded by a community of fellow dreamers. As we share our stories, laughter mingles with the clinking of glasses, and support flows like the local rosé, making me feel part of something bigger.

With their encouragement, I weave together the threads of my first novel, the characters coming alive with each word. A sense of pride blooms within me; I am no longer just a writer but a storyteller, and I realise the transformative power of storytelling. This newfound confidence pushes me to book a tour of the Camargue, where the flamingos and white horses thrive.

The tour of the Camargue is a journey of discovery, a reflection of my transformation. It's there that I meet Mark, and at that moment, another chapter of the adventure begins.

The ferry rocks gently beneath us as darkness falls. Mark is leaning against the railing, his laughter mingling with the sound of the waves. His eyes sparkle, drawing me in as we talk about everything and nothing.

As the hours slip away at sea, I glimpse the weight he carries – the shadows under his smile and the occasional pause in his voice. He speaks of the French countryside, his words painting vivid images of rolling hills and quiet villages, starkly contrasting the burden he bears at home. I can understand his longing to escape to that beauty, as I yearned for it myself.

Despite my lingering attraction towards him, I find comfort in our conversation. We share stories and dreams, and the exchange weaves a bond that is more profound than either of us expected, a bond that our shared French adventures strengthen.

As the ferry approaches the dock, the sun rises over the Spinnaker tower, signalling the journey's close. I feel a bittersweet sense of anticipation. Whatever the future has in store for me, Mark, or us, I feel assured that a new chapter is being crafted. I promise to stay connected – a spark of something new igniting between us, potentially waiting patiently for the right time to flourish.

I awaken hours later, and over the days and weeks that follow, I have come to understand that the final piece of the puzzle is me. My butterflies flutter within me as my heart swells with pride.

I glance at the stack of notebooks beside me, each page filled with characters waiting to leap off the paper. How many stories are yet to be born? So many ideas flutter just beneath the surface, itching to be released.

Ruth's voice is a guiding beacon in my creative journey. She echoes in my mind, urging me to dive deeper and commit fully to this passion. I can feel the urgency pulsing through my veins

– this is my moment. I close my eyes, envisioning the worlds I will create and the characters I will bring to life.

I take a deep breath, feeling the weight of possibility. It's time to pursue this calling, to let my imagination soar beyond the confines of the everyday.

As I sit at my desk, the manuscript before me is no longer just pages of words – it's a map of my journey. Ruth's notes in the margins still make me smile, each suggestion a stepping stone to becoming the writer I want to be.

My phone buzzes – a message from Mark. 'Thinking of you. How's the revising going?'

I hesitate, fingers hovering over the keys. We've been texting occasionally since the ferry crossing. Nothing serious, nothing committed, just... connection. I'm not sure where it's heading, if anywhere. And for the first time, that uncertainty no longer frightens me.

'Slow but rewarding,' I reply. 'Still figuring out my ending.'

That is true of both my novel and my life. I don't have all the answers yet. The woman who desperately wired money to Turkey is gone. So is the woman who ran from Barry's affection. Who I am now is still emerging, page by page, day by day.

I look at the framed quote above my desk, one I chose after returning from France:

'The butterfly counts not months but moments and has time enough.

Time enough for mistakes, for growth, for second chances – or third, or fourth.

Time enough to become.'

LOVE, LIES AND BUTTERFLIES

'The **love** I have for my family, friends, and life itself knows no bounds; it is an unwavering force that fuels my spirit. The **lies** that once clouded my journey are now firmly behind me, transformed into powerful tales of resilience and growth. I have emerged stronger, with my heart open wide. And now, the **butterflies** within me are bursting free, ready to spread their wings and soar into a future brimming with endless possibilities.

About the Author

Three years ago, I took a leap of faith and embarked on my writing journey after dedicating 40 years to the finance world. It was a significant shift, but oh, how it has transformed my life! My first series of self-published children's books draws inspiration from the incredible animals and dedicated staff I encountered while volunteering at Animal Rescue. Reflecting on this journey, I realise how much I've grown—not just as a writer, but as a person. Each story I crafted allowed me to explore new facets of my identity and the world around me. Over time, my appreciation for the craft of writing stories and the business has deepened. And I've set my sights on a new goal: to write stories for adults—both fiction and nonfiction. My first endeavour is a heartfelt short story about my mother, born in Bermondsey, London, at the dawn of World War II.

This project has been a beautiful journey of discovery, allowing me to learn more about her and connect with my family history.

This journey has been a mix of wonder and challenge, but my passion for writing shines brighter than ever. I am grateful to be part of this magical profession. Drawing on the support of my incredible family, valuable contacts, and resilient self-belief, I'm now pleased to bring you my first adult fiction novel. Love, Lies and Butterflies

Read more at www.Christineskippinsauthor.com.

www.ingramcontent.com/pod-product-compliance
Ingram Content Group UK Ltd.
Pitfield, Milton Keynes, MK11 3LW, UK
UKHW041539040925
462559UK00002B/25